Frank Cowan

Zomara

A romance of Spain

Frank Cowan

Zomara
A romance of Spain

ISBN/EAN: 9783337245542

Printed in Europe, USA, Canada, Australia, Japan

Cover: Foto ©Andreas Hilbeck / pixelio.de

More available books at **www.hansebooks.com**

Yours Truly
Frank Cowan

ZOMARA.

A Romance of Spain.

BY

FRANK COWAN.

———

PITTSBURGH, PA.
1873.

ZOMARA.

COME, gather around this cheerful fire, my children and my children's children, and listen to my Christmas story—a tale of the olden time, of that land of romance and fable—Spain.

Some tale of the Cid?

Santiago! and Compostella!

Another Alhambra?

Toledos trusty

Bull-fights!

The inquisition!

Don Quixote! Gil Blas!

Dons! Duennas! Darkness! Dungeons! Daggers!

Fandangos!

Castles in Spain!

Walking Spanish!

Tut! tut! my children, one and all; let not your imaginations run away with you at the mere mention of a name; and Tommy, with your "Walking Spanish"—no satire, if you please, in the guise of innocence.

Castile soap!—said Tommy, with even more severity than before.

Irrepressible!—Well, Tommy, it is Christmas eve, and I forgive you. Now, take the leg of your stool off Tabby's tail, and let me begin.

I.

IT was a stormy Christmas morning. Zomara, a young soldier, brave, courteous, generous, and handsome—a hero in reality, and may be not degenerate in fiction—landed in a little but ancient seaport town on the southern coast of Spain—in fine, in the grand old kingdom of Grenada. With difficulty he landed, for the sea was running high, and the shore was ragged with rocks. But seven weary days and nights had he been baffled by the winds and waves in his endeavor to reach this port before noon on Christmas-day, and, however dangerous the venture, by adroitly steering into a narrow inlet between two jutting rocks, and riding on the back of a monstrous wave, he reached a snug little cove of safety. Leaving his lieutenant in charge of the boat, he proceeded alone into the town.

Haste was evident, not only in his hurried step, but in his eager eye—he looked here, he looked there, to find somebody to direct his course. But he looked in vain. The streets of the old town were as bare of human life as if the storm that swept through them was the breath of a plague. And a shudder seized the soldier, as, in turning a corner, he suddenly ran against a body, lying on the ground, to all appearances a corpse.

But the seemingly dead man, awakened by the concussion from the stupor of drunkenness, rose, after several futile attempts, to a sitting posture, uncertain and vacillating, but erect enough to extend his circle of ambiguous vision to include the presence of one or more individuals.

Ho! Pedro! another pull at the flagon!—hiccoughed the drunken man.

My good fellow,—said Zomara,—it is not your comrade Pedro, but a soldier tossed on the stormy sea till—

Who's at sea?

And half seas over, you might add, with the same breath, if your hiccoughing did not break it too short,—continued Zomara. But,—growing impatient,—I am in great haste—I would see Don Altanero, of Grenada—can you direct me to his mansion?

Now, this drunken man was the butler—yes, butler will do—of Don Altanero himself, and the mention of his master's name had a magic effect in restoring his wandering senses; and that prerogative of man, reason, was brought into play, though in a confused manner. A soldier—a stranger—wants to see my master—in haste—a very unusual occurrence—must mislead the inquirer—and stagger home as fast as I can, and warn my master—and on the heels of duty, crave forgiveness for this drunken bout.

Stranger,—said the butler, whose name I may here tell you was Martin,—stranger, do you see that massive gate at the foot of this street—the gate to the right—no, left—which is my right hand?—yes, to the right. Go there.

Zomara hurried down the street to the gate indicated, and knocked. He knocked again and again, with increasing violence and impatience. He was about to burst it open in despair, when a voice at his shoulder said—

You'll rap at that gate long, before you'll be answered from within—you rap at the gate of the city of the dead—the cemetery—where sleep Christian and Moor side by side for a thousand years—their warfare over—in eternal peace.

That voice familiar,—said Zomara turning, and clasping in his warm embrace a friend of long standing, a college chum at a German university, a companion at court at Madrid before they separated, one to go into the army, the other to return to his father's princely estate here in Grenada.

What, my good friend, Alvaro! and reflective and philosophic as ever. Well, I am glad to find that you are not within these walls, at peace with Christian and Turk; for, if my memory serves me right, with your skeptical books and refined logic, you were at war with both when we were last together. But, pardon my abruptness, Alvaro, for I have but a few hours of freedom left, and I must see Don Altanero, who lives somewhere in this neighborhood.

If Altanero's magic name restored a drunken butler to reason and awakened a train of thoughts that led to a definite course of action, you must imagine what it excited in the brain of a studious, observing, and reflective man, remarkable for possessing these qualities in a rare degree, who was at that moment as much more interested in Don Altanero as differed the philosopher from the drunken fool—you must, with the lively imagination you set out with, picture his crowding, rushing, concentrating and diverging thoughts; I cannot utter them. But how came he to be so intensely interested in the old Don at that particular time? I will tell you. Don Altanero, despite his poverty and pride, the usual accompaniments of high life for several successive generations in as well as out of Spain—despite his tolerable poverty and intolerable pride, Don

Altanero had a daughter, Isabel, the most beautiful and accomplished young lady in Grenada. Take this for granted; I am too old to go into details. And Alvaro, the son of Borracho, the richest old Don in Grenada, and a friend and neighbor, in the full sense of those words, to Altanero,—well, of course, Alvaro fell in love with Isabel, and proposed to sue for her hand that very Christmas-day, the anniversary of her nineteenth natal day, the occasion of a birthday party at Altanero's; and he was just then loitering in the footsteps of his father, sent before to negotiate with the father of his intended bride. It flashed across Alvaro's mind accordingly, like a calcium light, that scorched as it lit up every thing with dazzling brightness, that, during a winter's stay of Isabel at Madrid, there was an intimacy between Zomara and Isabel. Then again, like lightning that blighted in its momentary course, flashed upon him the situation—Zomara seeking Altanero—seeking Isabel, with but a few hours of freedom left; but long enough, with bravery, wealth, title, worth, to press his suit, favored by Isabel, most probably successfully! Suspicion aroused a tiger that rent him in twain, and tore his very vitals in agony!

But a few hours of freedom left?—why, Zomara, what can this mean?—asked Alvaro, with feigned amazement?

Alas! that I should herald my disgrace!

Disgrace!

Banished—

Banished!

Banished for a father's alleged apostacy. This Christmas-day at noon begins my term of exile. A wanderer in foreign lands for two years must I be—chains and death—ignominy the alternative!

A terrible doom.

But, reasoned Alvaro, this is a severe penalty for a father's apostacy. The excuse is lame. There must be treason back of it. The powerful house of Zomara of Castile has long been regarded with suspicion. And now he would not only consummate his intimacy with Isabel by obtaining her hand, but league with him Altanero, though with wasted revenues, the leading political nobleman in

the south of Spain! Here, then, is the destiny not only of Alvaro, but perhaps, also, of Spain! He must be detained till after twelve to-day, then arrested, and carried in chains to the king—or die! for the oath of my life has been, Isabel shall be mine, and I will not perjure my soul for a personal rival, and a traitor to my country!

At this juncture Martin came staggering along, hiccoughing duty—duty—duty.

What!—exclaimed Zomara,—here is the drunken knave that bade me knock at this cemetery gate. It is tolerable the wrath of a sovereign, and to be thwarted by storms, but to be the gibe of an intoxicated varlet, a reeling buffoon, passes all endurance!

Aha! and Martin is suspicious too?—thought Alvaro,—I have it. Martin shall still direct him, since he has made such a good beginning.

Martin!—said Alvaro, catching the staggering butler by the neck, and straightening him up to the rigidity of sensibility and clear comprehension,—Martin, you are not too drunk to conduct this gallant soldier aright, nor too drunk to understand a threat of broken bones if you fail. He is in haste to see your master. Farewell, Zomara; urgent business prevents my accompanying you myself; success attend your mission,—and, turning coldly and abruptly, he left his old friend in amaze at his treatment of him, and disappeared in a moment on turning into a neighboring narrow alley.

II.

WHILE Martin is leading Zomara by the nose, as he intended, and as you may suppose, if you please, let us go into Don Altanero's house, and see what is doing there by way of celebrating, at the same time, the anniversary of Isabel's natal day and Christmas.

In the early morning Don Borracho, the rich and generous old friend and neighbor of Altanero, and the father of Alvaro, you will remember, sent a basket of fine wines and rich viands to Altanero, in response to the latter's invitation to join in the festive celebration of the day. And the bearer of this basket of luxuries was Pedro—he for whom Martin called when aroused from stupor to dreams, midway to comprehension of external objects and reason—he from whom Martin filched the bottle of wine that made him so gloriously tight. Now this Pedro, you must know; for as the attendant of Borracho, he will figure throughout the story.

Physically, Pedro was long, lank, and leathery-looking; while, mentally, he resembled the shadow of philosophy reflected from a rippling brook. He was neat and precise in his dress to a point approaching foolish; serious and grave—nay, severe in his aspect; but, with a prominent ruby-tinted nose between his leather-like lantern jaws, the ludicrous hypocrite that he was, was plainly discernible in his visage. He was in love, too—if the liking of a cold-blooded animal, warmed into activity only by wine, can be included in that term. And the object of his batrachian affection was Nona, a matronly, middle-aged waiting-maid, seared, soured, and rheumatic, in the household of Altanero—a female whose charms had also made an impression on the heart of Martin, good-natured, rollicking, reveling Martin, now having Zomara in charge.

Ah, Pedro, this bottle is far from being full, and the cork is very loose,—said Nona, suspicious, as she and Pedro were arranging the contents of Borracho's Christmas basket on the sideboard.

That is strange, very strange,—quietly remarked Pedro.—Let me examine it,—and, of course, before he got through with his examination, he had, when the opportune moment arrived, further reduced the tide of the contents, and to a very low ebb. The bottle must leak,—he said, sagely, as he placed it with great deliberation on the board where he could not mistake it.

But don't you think, Pedro, that if Alvaro would offer himself to Isabel, his suit would be accepted? and the match hailed with—confound this stormy weather, it makes my bones ache,—said Nona, recurring to a theme she had been harping on all morning, until Pedro's swigging, or her rheumatic twinges, brought her to an abrupt termination.

Well, well, Nona,—said Pedro,—a woman's a woman the wide world over—inquisitive to the marrow. I do think these two ancient houses should be, and will be, united, Alvaro and Isabel, Pedro and —

And who?—curtly asked Nona.—Out, out, you sanctimonious, soaking saphead!—or words to that effect, for it must not be supposed that I give her exact expressions.—Begone, you leathery, lantern-jawed lout! La me! a pretty match! to marry a man who spends his time in gaping and guzzling! Heigho! If Isabel doesn't marry Alvaro before I do you, she'll rise thrice from her grave and dance in a shroud at her wed—confound this stormy weather, say I. Pedro, don't you know what is good for the rheumatism?

I do,—said Pedro, gravely; and suiting his action to his concealed intent, deliberately extended his long arms, like the tentacles of a cuttlefish, encircled the frame racked with rheumatism, and pressed it to his bosom with a feeling that would have done credit to a locust post.

Now, if there was one thing, one principle, or axiom that formed the basis of Pedro's philosophy, and not only formed the basis, but rose the uppermost and most frequent pinnacle of his belief, it was—a woman's a woman the wide world over. And, of course, he gave utterance to his philosophic convictions on this occasion, when he found that Nona, in spite of her rheumatic joints, limbered with alacrity, and acquiesced in the embrace in a very satisfactory manner. He was about to add, moreover, that there was no remedy known, from the time of Galen to his own, that was so efficacious with female patients afflicted with rheumatism, or even lumbago, as hugging, when he was broken off by Nona, still further furnishing proof of the truth of his aphorism, by exclaiming—

Pedro! Pedro! there's somebody coming!

And sure enough, and before the deliberate Pedro could unwind his tentacles, and restore himself to his stoic equanimity and insensibility, Don Altanero, the haughty and the exacting, in accordance with his poverty and pride, entered the room, in a serious and thoughtful—nay, severe mood!

You will remember that term of your chemistry, catalysis—the effect of one agent on another simply by its presence. Now, if you wish to treat this matter like savants, in a truly scientific way, please consider the effect produced by Altanero's presence on Pedro and Nona as that of catalysis, and pronounce the experiment in this parlor laboratory a beautiful success. For without uttering a word, or paraphrasing Pedro's aphorism with—a varlet's a varlet the wide world over, Altanero quietly crossed the floor, and Nona skipped off in one direction, in a very lively manner, considering her rheumatism and the condition of the weather, and Pedro shuffled off in the other, with his usual ghost-like solemnity, but with an unusual reflection of the ruddy hue of his nose illuminating his lantern jaws.

III.

THE truth is, Altanero was in a brown study at that particular time, about himself, his family, and his affairs, and he could ignore, and did, such minor objects as a valet and a waiting-maid. A brown study, did I say? A blue or a black would be a more appropriate color, for the old Don—to use your familiar phrase—had the blues, and, contradictorily enough, too, the world looked black, very black to him.

It is not very probable that he soliloquized aloud, and gave utterance to his thoughts and feelings in words; but if he had, he would have spoken with this effect,—for the circumstances pointed directly to this end—

This day my daughter Isabel attains her nineteenth year. It is a day of rejoicing and congratulation. She is the only child of the ancient house of Altanero—a noble line from the conquest down—and in her concentrate all hopes of its proud continuance. But, alas! what poor and paltry decorations are these, and dearth of generous food and wine, for a festive occasion of so much significance as this! Curses on the fate that compels such faint and feeble rejoicings on her natal day! But what's this?—observing the viands and wines that Pedro and Nona had displayed to good advantage on the sideboard.

There needs no card to indicate the source of this generous gift. Ha! neighbor and friend, rich Borracho, your bounty has so richly filled this board. Rich Borracho—and poor Altanero! Withering contrast, breeding envy, hatred and malice for him I must admire and love for his good, generous, and noble qualities—and riches! Ah, misery, misery, the constant contest of a scant purse to furnish out the appearance of a lord—till relieved with supplies from the coffers of a wealthy neighbor!

There is no telling how far the reaction of his haughty spirit would have carried the harrowed Don—whether to the demolition of the wine bottles with a hasty blow of his truculent cane, or merely to the emptying of one, in the only true and legitimate business way, direct from the bottle to the holder, without the intervention of a middle-man goblet. But no matter to conjecture; for the arrival of Don Borracho himself, open and impetuous, and burdened with the mission of his son, which he was anxious to relieve himself of, made such a change in the affairs of Altanero that the thoughts he was tormented with at that time were banished into the gloom of the past, and in their stead gleamed hopes of a bright future.

Ah, ha! my old comrade! a merry Christmas to you!—roared out the jovial, generous Borracho, as he entered the room.—A happy Christmas, Altanero; and a century of repetitions for both of us! But, my lord, what mean these downcast looks? I looked not to see the scowl of the storm without invade this happy hall on an occasion like this. Cheer up, my lord; cheer up, old friend.

Welcome, Borracho,—replied Altanero, his repelling reserve relaxing and metamorphosing into hearty hospitality,—as a loathsome larva, with a twitch and a jerk, sunders its repulsive case, and emerges a chrysalid, mottled with deftly contrasted colors, and flecked with gold.

Welcome, generous friend; your face would drive away the heaviest clouds and bless the house with warmth and light. And a happy Christmas to you and yours, from the depth of my heart. Aye, and thanks, too, for the generous gift this morning.

Thanks! thanks!—exclaimed Borracho, with mock amazement and horror.—The deuce take such thanks! Come, pledge me with a bumper. An old man traveling through the winds this morning requires something more invigorating than words! Pedro! Pedro! Come, old snail, some wine!

And Pedro, fully restored to philosophic serenity and owl-like sapiency, stalked, with ludicrous precision and solemnity, from a recess, and filled two goblets to the brim.

Pedro! Pedro! I'll punch a hole through your cobwebs with this cane, that will let daylight into you if not activity!—cried out his impatient master.

Here's to the health,—began Altanero.

Drink first,—said Borracho, interrupting him unceremoniously.—Drink first, and we'll have the rest of the day to talk about it afterward.

A side issue,—soliloquized Pedro, as he joined the Dons, behind their backs, from the leaky bottle.

Now for business,—said Borracho, bustling about, and offering a chair to Altanero, as if he were host instead of guest.—And, Pedro,—beans in your ears and the lockjaw, if you remain, else withdraw.

But Pedro, refreshed, chose rather to retire where he could hear probably just as well, and, at the same time, with Noua, comment and communicate without restraint, and add additional proof to the truth of his dogma, that a woman's a woman the wide world over.

Now for business,—said Borracho again.—Egad, Altanero, I have come with weighty mission. Ha! these young folks make their sires their servants. Know, then, Don Altanero, of Grenada, of the Order of the Golden Fleece—

Golden Fleece?—said Altanero, quizzically;—no satire, I hope.

What, quibbling already, and in business? Why, I'll have you hanged—no; that would honor and dignify the gallows too much; I'll have you drowned in wine, to lend it ever after an additional sparkle! And that reminds me,—Pedro! Pedro! some more wine, this stormy morning.

And Pedro was not long in answering the summons. He was as bibulous as his master, and as loath to go far from the bottle. So helping the Dons and himself, as before, he retired again.

Now for business—the third attempt; and may this third time not disprove the proverb that therein lies the charm of success,—began Borracho again.—Now, you must know, Don Altanero, that my most sovereign son and master, Don Alvaro, ripe in years, studies, accomplishments and means, for what he proposes, sends his most unworthy father and servant, Don Borracho—myself! Egad, think of it!—as envoy extraordinary, with full powers to treat for the hand of your gentlest, fairest, sweetest daughter Isabel.

Alvaro seeks the hand of Isabel?—said Altanero, with feigned astonishment, for, to tell you the truth, he had long looked for this as a possibility, satisfactory to him in every particular.

Yes,—added Borracho;—and, faith, his hot impatience tarries but little behind my tardy speech. So, blurting out the truth, I have hurried with my tongue to lead his haste. But a little business mars my palate's taste. Will you consent to this marriage?

Make haste slowly,—said Altanero, reflectingly. —Let me think awhile.

But it did not take him long to consider the fitness of the match. That Alvaro was the able and learned son of a house as ancient and as famous as his own, and the sole heir of a princely estate, with increasing revenues, he was well aware; as he was also that a friendship existed between Alvaro and Isabel from their childhood, for he himself had fostered a neighborly acquaintance to that point. But, as he was well assured that concealed satisfaction would better secure success, he kept his real thoughts beneath the surface.

You forget,—at length said Altanero to the envoy extraordinary,—I hold no power from Isabel to treat with you on this important matter. Has Alvaro any assurances that his suit will be acceptable and accepted by Isabel herself; for I am not so unfeeling to the happiness of that which is dearest to me on earth, my daughter, as to ignore it in this treaty?

He doubts it not, nor do I,—answered Borracho. —But what do you think?

It is true,—said Altanero,—that they have lived from childhood as neighbors and friends, and it is not improbable that if the thistle-like seeds of love, that are wafted hither and thither, no man knows where,—it is not improbable that those seeds that have fallen and grown to maturity in the heart of Alvaro, should have been borne also into the bosom of Isabel, and at least taken root there. I will not oppose my daughter's—nay, our children's wishes—they should move a parent's heart. But here's Pedro with wine,—the blotter had concluded his time to absorb again had arrived, —let us fill to the brim and drain to the bottom, and close this diplomatic conference with a health to the happiness of those whom our labors bring together. A long life to them, and a pleasant one to us.

I thank you,—said Borracho, draining his cup to the dregs.—I have long loved Isabel as my own child, and now she will be mine indeed. Ah! this marriage brings up the days of yore, when, with fair words to the ladies and sure swords with our rivals, we won and lost—when hearts were trumps. Egad! but spades will soon turn up, and tell us of another trump!—which is pretty good proof that the jovial old Don was not unacquainted with the mysteries and delights of the deck.

Ha! ha! good,—added Altanero, appreciating the figure and allusion from an evident acquaintance, if not familiarity, with the game. And,— not forgetting the plans broached that jumped so happily with his desires,—I shall inform my daughter to-day of the result of our conference, that the lovers the sooner may see their wishes fulfilled. The anniversary of her birthday, too— the very time. But, here come the ladies.

IV.

ADY MARIANA, the wife of Altanero, Isabel, the daughter, Teresa, Isabel's governess and confidante, with a score of guests and several attendants, entered the room.

After a general congratulation as the occasion required, a Christmas morn, and the anniversary of Isabel's birthday, Altanero approached his daughter, the centre about which all revolved, and saluted her with a bow gracious with kindness and approving satisfaction at her womanly worth.

Pardon the pride,—said he,—of a fond father, who as 'twere but yesterday danced the child upon his knee, and now beholds a noble woman stand before him—the hope concentrate of a house mature—the link well wrought that extends the ancient family of Altanero one remove farther in the annals of time.

My dear father,—said Isabel, with a keen appreciation of her father's words, and a feeling that responded to this apparent overflowing of his affection for her,—you are ever kind and affectionate to me; and grateful as I am for the care, protection, and nurture shown the child, I trust the years of my maturity may serve to smooth the path and make happy the lives of those whom I so dearly love and owe so much.

Our Gracious Lady guide you, Isabel,—said her mother, deeply imbued with a religious feeling and fervor that found expression not only in words but in acts of charity and love to all at all times, —Our Gracious Lady guide you, and guard you from the sorrows and cares which attend on years of responsibility.

But cares will come to all, my lady,—said Borracho to the pious mother,—but when they do come to our daughter—

Our daughter?—significant, my lord,—said Altanero, with a knowing look, to his friend.

Yes; to our daughter,—continued Borracho,— may they come lightly, and, the proverb be fulfilled, as lightly go.

But what delays our son, old friend?—asked Altanero, continuing his knowing looks, and adding to them pith and point with a deliberate wink, that not only closed his left eye, but gave a gentle movement to his left ear, which—not to speak it irreverently of the haughty old Don—gave him a conical expression for once in his life,—I think our son should be here by this.

And he is, even as you speak.

Alvaro betrayed his excitement the very moment he entered; but his father and Altanero attributed it to the occasion and its significance to him, and thought little about it. But there was one within that room that looked with the intensity of her very soul through a dark, deep and yet flashing eye, that saw in his emotion something that blanched her olive face, and made her being shrivel and contract within itself, till it stood an imperturbed point. That one was Teresa—the governess of Isabel, a woman her senior by ten years; misfortune and poverty—so she said—brought her to Don Altanero's several years ago; and she had been retained for her worth as an instructor, guide, and confidante to Isabel ever since. Yes; it was Teresa that took this look of intensity—one look, and brief as a glance, lest its continuance or repetition, should blaze into fire, consume her into ashes, and at the same instant dart through the soul of Alvaro like the arrow of Acestes or a lightning bolt. One glance only she took, and that unseen by any; then turned and withdrew herself into an individuality whose presence there was known in its reality only to herself.

I beg your pardon,—said Alvaro, addressing Altanero,—and fair ladies, for my tardiness. But on my way I met, to be detained in talking of his cares, a friend—

Be brief, my son,—said Borracho.—We'll hear of your friend at some other time. Our host, Don Altanero, would speak.

And now one word about Zomara, whom we left a few minutes ago in the company of Martin, the drunken butler. The instant Alvaro turned the corner and disappeared in the alley, a suspicion entered the soldier's mind, and he determined to follow him at all hazards; so to dispose of the troublesome Martin, who seemed determined to cling to him for support and detention, he gave him an impatient push that laid him on the broad of his back, then followed as quickly and as quietly as he could in the steps of the retreating Alvaro, and entered the unguarded door of Altanero's mansion close upon his heels, crossed the hall, and gained the door of the parlor as Alvaro ceased speaking, where he could, unobserved, see much and hear all, and where, accordingly, he chose to remain till he became acquainted with the situation, which was not long.

My friends and guests,—began Altanero,—we are gathered together to celebrate the holy anniversary of the natal day of Jesus, the Anointed, Blessed Son of the Holy Virgin, to whom, with profound veneration, we bend the humbled head, and symbolize the cross, upon which He was crucified for our salvation, upon our breasts,—the earnest expression and deep reverence of which exordium cast a serious gloom over the whole assembly, and found responsive action in all.

We are here, also, to rejoice and give thanks,—he continued,—that it has pleased the Most High to bestow upon us, unworthy as we are, upon this blessed day, a daughter who fills the measure of our hopes and desires,—directing the attention of all to Isabel in a solemn and impressive manner.

And we are here,—he added, in the same earnest tones,—to rejoice in plans by which her future is assured, an ancient name increased in lustre, by the happy union of two houses, not unknown or unhonored in this proud land,—bowing, with dignity, to Borracho, and exciting all with an intense interest, which in several was agonizing, as the purport of this speech flashed upon them—Isabel, Zomara, and Teresa.

Isabel stood breathless as a statue, with surprise, uncertainty, and woe depicted in her blanched face.

Teresa leaned forward with an eagerness that threatened to topple her on the floor, while the throbbing of her heart, in the death-like stillness that prevailed, fell upon her ear like the knell of hope and the footfall of despair.

While Zomara, already wrought with disappointment and baffled aims to a pitch of excitement almost uncontrollable, his bosom heaving with emotions roused by the sight of Isabel, and under such racking circumstances, dropped his forehead, beaded with perspiration, into the hollow of his hand, and felt the first moment of despair of his life.

Dear Isabel,—continued Altanero,—now that age comes apace on us, your first protectors, it is our desire that Don Alvaro, your friend and neighbor from infancy, an honorable gentleman, of acknowledged worth and renown, should succeed us in that care, and, as your husband, soon assume still higher duties and more tender offices. Alvaro,—taking Isabel's hand, and, disregarding its deathlike coldness and insensibility, about to place it in Alvaro's,—Alvaro, Isabel is yours for life.

Unable to restrain his bursting passion and emotions in silence and inaction any longer, Zomara strode into the room with that mighty majesty that belongs alone to man when his physical forces are strained to the highest pitch, and yet obedient to a mental master, cool, courageous, and determined as death itself. Walking directly to Altanero, and spreading consternation at every step, he parted the inanimate Isabel and the astonished Alvaro, and uttered those words, that sent a thrill of awe to the hearts of all in the room,—No! no! this cannot be! Betrothed to me, she is mine, and must remain, unless absolved by death or revocation of her vows by her unfettered will. Speak, Isabel! by the bonds of sweet communion and affection—the sacred pledge by which I have lived since last we met ; speak, Isabel, and tell the world that our lives, bound by holy ties, are one; speak, by the love you bear me, and by your faith in God; oh! speak, and dissipate the cloud which closes round and stifles hope.

Zomara! Zomara!—exclaimed Isabel, now master of herself and the situation, an independent factor to make and not be altogether moved and moulded by circumstances,—your presence here is a fearful, but a blessed interposition. I revoke not the words—

But Alvaro would hear no more ; a brave, headstrong, willful man, he was not to be balked by a rival, and submit in silence ; especially when he felt that not only the might of the united heads of the Borracho and Altanero households was with him, but the power of the Spanish realm itself would unite with him to hunt down the traitor, as he supposed him, to the death.

Demon of discord,—cried out Alvaro, lashing himself into a rage and fury, that knew no bounds, and respected no society,—devil incarnate, to enter where all was peace. Rash man, how dare you assert rights here, when you are now a felon unfettered, a traitor untrammeled, only by the sufferance of your one time dearest friend ?

The uniform I wear,—said Zomara, with a majestic utterance that plainly showed his unmoved courage,—by loyalty and bravery won, explains or justifies my presence here, or elsewhere in the Spanish realm.

Dog, you lie!—exclaimed Alvaro.—Treason to the State has banished you this realm. The hour of twelve to-day dooms you to a felon's grave. Ha! and hark! that hour has arrived! the clock is ringing your knell!

Treason!—cried several.

Arrest the traitor!—cried Altanero.

Down with the dog!—cried Borracho.

Yield, traitor!—demanded Alvaro, in a stern voice, advancing with a firm step.

That term suffices!—said Zomara, his anger ablaze, his neck swelling, and his veins rising like welts.—The hour of twelve is past. My life on Spanish ground is now my king's, but not for treason ; and to my king alone will I yield it !—Pardon, fair ladies. And if you are, base, treacherous Alvaro, what dress and fortune, and not your record shows, a man, with right and heart to wear and wield a sword, then draw, and prove with life or brave defence thereof, your right thus to upbraid me, one by rank your equal and by prowess mayhap more !

And the clash of swords in another instant rang through the halls of the old mansion, increasing to a fearful degree the excitement and confusion, with its echoing clangor. Ladies and attendants were fleeing in affright. Lady Mariana swooned on the floor, and lay with none to attend her. Borracho and Altanero, with the hot blood of youth, and their plans so disastrously defeated, were eager to join the affray with their canes. But Teresa, wringing her hands in wild despair, watched every thrust and parry and lunge, with an intensity of interest that would have betrayed her at any other moment, but now all eyes were on the furious combatants. And Isabel—then it was that the heroic spirit, that had spurred on her ancestors for centuries to glory, rose within her and manifested itself in a courage and a comprehension, during the wildest excitement, that belongs only to the highest types of mankind.

The match was not an unequal one; nor was it the first time the combatants had crossed blades, but the first in deadly strife. And the combat gave evidence of a protracted trial of skill, when suddenly, an adroit lunge of Zomara's scored Alvaro's neck and slit his ear, drawing the first blood; and in an instant after, both stood at sword-point at rest.

Restrain rash hands,—said Isabel, boldly stepping between the combatants, with a determination and a defiance commanding the most impetuous,—let not your raging rivalry break down the fair, brave citadel of life, and sorrow send to many loving hearts. Alvaro, if you have my father's favor, and dare hope for mine, return your sword into its sheath. And oh, Zomara, leave this hostile place, and trust that God, who gave our love, will yet fulfill its dearest hopes!

Begone, you treason-tainted villain,—exclaimed Altanero, chagrined again to the core at this declaration of love by Isabel for one he supposed to be but a passing acquaintance, at most a friend,—begone, before I anticipate the law's righteous doom. Use well your time. Presume to place your feet within these walls again, and, by the name I bear, your life shall not escape my wrath. And, Isabel, to your chamber.

At her entreaty,—replied Zomara,—not at your commands and threats, I leave a place where nothing but love for Isabel can lead me to return. But, haughty man, beware how far you force that girl to bend to your imperious will. Dare cause a pang to her,—cross her path with tyranny and cruelty, instead of a father's kindness and love, and your walls and slaves shall be as straw to retain this brightest jewel in Spain's diadem. Dear Isabel, adieu!

Farewell! farewell!—cried Isabel; and before she could add a word of hope or cheer, as she intended, Zomara had passed rapidly through the door by which he entered the house, and Martin, not restored to sobriety yet, came staggering in at an opposite door, muttering duty—duty—my lord—beware of the traitor!—and such like broken sentences that would indubitably prove his fidelity to his master, and in the most trying circumstances. But Martin was not long in comprehending the circumstances, and his stupid folly, when he saw the confusion of everything; saw the blood trickling down Alvaro's neck, and felt a blow across his shoulders with the back of his sword that sent him reeling against the sideboard, and scattering Borracho's generous gift of viands and wines on the floor.

V.

ISABEL and Teresa retired to their chamber, the former with a hurried, but a firm step, the latter faltering, uncertain, and lagging behind.

Banished, said he?

He did.

For two years?

Two years—the term beginning at noon to-day. His life is forfeited?—

To the king.

After this brief dialogue, Isabel, excited to a pitch that kept her in constant motion, walking to and fro, resolved in her mind the various phases of the situation, and with great deliberation and determination decided on a course of action.

Teresa.

What will you, my lady?

You must seek—must find Zomara, without delay. He will flee the town and country at the first opportunity. Haste you must have. While the house is in confusion, your absence will be unobserved—go—oh, go, Teresa! I must see him!—The mention of Zomara's name, and the expression of her desire to see him, awakening an emotion that bid her determination hesitate, falter, and finally yield—the heart of the noble woman asserting its supremacy over the head.

But where would you see him?

Where? Here! anywhere!

Not to meet his fate, my lady?

Ah, no, Teresa; to live, to—

And then one tear after the other rolled down her cheek, blanched now to a marble whiteness, that a few minutes before was flushed and full—one pearl after another, that were such treasures hoarded in the bottom of the sea, no depth or danger would deter the daring diver in his search for them.

But as Isabel gave way to her emotions, Teresa recovered her wonted serenity and deep contemplation, till a series of thoughts in rapid succession lapped and folded over one and the other, till a perfect pyramid was formed in her mind, having for its base, as immovable as granite itself, the fact,—Alvaro shall not marry Isabel whilst Teresa lives!—and thence upward to a pointed apex,—nor other than Teresa!—If the one, Isabel, was the superior mentally of the other in moments of excitement, danger and terror, the other, Teresa, was the greater by far in the long, still hours that make up so much of a woman's existence; and years of brooding in silence over her sorrow—her mingled love and woe, had grooved the latter's thoughts that they waited but for the accustomed solitude to resume their wonted course. Teresa accordingly determined that Isabel must not be a rival; and to make this a fixed fact, her affection for Zomara, now so publicly declared, must be accepted—nurtured—furthered to consummation! and in spite of dangers that may be death! for should she shrink from and shirk possibilities, when an existence worse a thousand fold than death is at stake, a fact, an agonizing reality!

My lady, I will see Zomara. I will appoint a tryst—time and place, best assurances of safety. Leave it to me.

Nay, stay, Teresa; consider the danger—the terrible risk! Two years will soon pass by—and then—

At your command, my lady.

Oh, no, no! Two years of vacillating between hope and despair after the scene of to-day, intolerable! Go, Teresa; this token give Zomara, in pledge of your mission of—love! of love! Oh, Teresa, am I a changed being that the word I trembled to whisper but yesterday, I should now utter with the intensity and fullness of my very soul? Go, Teresa; love will build such a wall about Zomara, that thrice the traitor he may be, the king himself cannot reach him.

Taking a ring from a little casket, hid in a secret recess in her dressing case, and kissing it several times with eager and ardent affection, Isabel handed it to Teresa, and bade her again go, and God speed—and then sank on her couch, and, as Teresa left her presence, burst into an unrestrained flood of tears.

Teresa, with a heavy mantle thrown over her shoulders, and a dark veil over her face, passed rapidly from one street to the other in search of Zomara; and shudder after shudder coursed through her as the angry storm winds, in fitful blasts, swept along; at one time nearly dashing her with violence against a wall, at another almost hurling her from her feet. But with every blast and lull without, the storm within the deeply feeling and thinking woman, was alternate—now reiterating, with increasing force, her determination, and now sinking into a calm of acceptance, coupled with keen appreciation, and culminating in mental misery.—Never—never must Alvaro wed another!—then,—Ah, woes thicken around my head! Alas, the misery to endure in silence slighted, blighted love! Alvaro—monster! and yet I love you, and will bear your cruelty, though woes thicken and darken around my head till the heaven of hope is shut out entirely. But never must you wed another!

And before she was gone an hour, she met the object of her search; for, after the defiance the soldier had given at the point of the sword the two most powerful houses in Grenada, he hesitated not to keep the open street, and took his own time

to reach the little cove where he had landed, and where his boat waited for him.

Zomara!

But Zomara paused before he followed the unknown and deeply-veiled woman under the lee of an ancient wall, where she led the way, to gain seclusion and shelter from the storm. He was not unfamiliar with the treachery of his fellow-men and women, and the subtle ruses resorted to, to attain an end. And yet there was such determination and directness in the action of the woman that could not be the accompaniment of design and villainy; and, after a moment's reflection, he stood by her side.

This ring be pledge of truth and security,—said Teresa.

Zomara took the ring, a heavy golden band, and, as he held it between his finger and thumb, his eye fell on two names engraved therein—Isabel—Zomara.

Isabel and Zomara,—he said;—two names separated, but united with a band of gold—two persons separated, but united with a band of love —a bond as much more precious than gold, as gold than the baser metals.

So would she that you would construe it.

Beloved symbol; I'll wear it next my heart, till torn from me, and I am not. Faithful friend, —with earnest, grateful tones, turning to Teresa, —the God of love reward you, watch over you, and bless you.

As love only can,—added Teresa,—make earth a heaven—or hell !—the latter escaping in audible words, which she intended should be but a whisper to her inner self.

And have you, too, felt that passion whose onward flow is bliss, and whose retarded motion or current checked is woe ?

The more faith, then, in my mission.

Aye, its object beyond this token—her message; impatience can endure silence no longer.

To-night, at twelve, meet her on the barren cliff in the rear of her father's mansion. Though the storm be running too high to venture in a boat, between the lashing wave and the base of the rock there is room enough for a brave man to travel,

though his stages from one point to the other be within the short periods of the influx of the wave, and his only light the faintly luminous crest of the foaming billow. Here you will be safe, and your interview may be protracted until dawn ; for he that dares the terrible storm of the elements at the base need fear no mortal power when he has scaled the cliff.

Ha ! ha ! good woman, you taunt me with your pictures of seeming danger !

But the king's decree may direct the dagger?

My life is forfeit to the king since noon to-day —ha ! a by-word and a jest henceforth !

Offended haughtiness of two noble houses—

I held at bay an hour ago, and chastised for presumption with a thrust that crimsoned the unworthy image of a man, and left a scar at which the finger of dishonor alone can point.

Man or monster may he be, but beware his revenge. Courage and might are his—a nod that nerves a hundred slaves, and a disregard that ruins a—

A confiding woman ! And fear the revenge of such a villain ? Taunt me no longer, good woman ; but return to the giver of this ring, and tell her, briefly, I will be there. No voucher have I but a soldier's word. Nay ; here is a pretty poignard, a trophy of my last encounter with the Italians. Ha ! I could be merry over such a token to my lady, but a soldier must do what he can, not what he would. And here's a crescent, set with pearls, taken in the wars with the Turks ; take this yourself, and wear it in remembrance of an exile's only bounty to one who has befriended him so much. Tell her, I will be on the cliff at midnight ; and I would burden this message with my love, but its weight would bear you down. Thanks, thanks, good woman ; adieu,—and Zomara disappeared as the command of an approaching guard fell with indistinctness on his ear, but with a significance unmistakable.

And Teresa, with the tokens in her hand, turned into the street, and returned to her mistress, musing the while—So goes the world even in these symbols: a dagger, image of death, to the innocent and pure—she who has but tasted of woe ; and a crescent, celestial image of brightness and hope, to her who has but tasted of happiness, and lived ever after in agony and despair. Ah! and a crescent, too, as if to taunt me with the Moorish blood that runs in my veins, separates me from the pure-blooded of Spain, and warrants Alvaro's desertion of me in the eyes of the world! Galling reminder! But I'll wear the symbol with pride, though I endure the reality with shame and despair!

VI.

ALVARO'S wrath and indignation, if possible, increased rather than diminished on reflection; and while yet the blood was flowing freely from his neck, he summoned the commandant of the guard of the town, and the command heard by Zomara already gave evidence of the celerity with which his orders were obeyed. But without avail; Zomara reached the little cove where his boat and men were in anxious waiting, and, despite the lashing waves, put out to sea at once to reach his vessel riding at anchor in the offing, though the swell of the sea threatened to snap the cable every instant; and, gaining the vessel in safety, put such a wall of waves between him and the shore, that no hireling guard, that too frequently trembled on solid ground, dared for a moment even the thought, much less the attempt, to cross.

But Zomara is gone, thought the thwarted Alvaro; and gone for two years, unless he dare defy the king and death in his hot rashness; and in that time how many sieges before the castle of the heart will be successful, and may not that of Isabel be of the number?

But this conclusion, however often arrived at, and by whatever ways, direct or devious, brought neither consolation nor satisfaction. He hurried to and fro in an excited and uncertain manner throughout the remainder of the day, unconscious of the stormy weather, or, if not, it was so like the storm within him that it was his most congenial element. And even into the night he wandered, till he found himself on the bleak cliff in the rear of Altanero's mansion, a lonely spot, wild and fearful in a calm day, but terrible in the extreme at the dead of night, with a roaring sea beneath, a storm rock above, and now and then a broad gleam of moonshine through the rifted heavens, like the grim smile of the storm god, quickly followed by the frown of dark clouds, and the lightning flashing anger from his eye!

The sublimity of the scene made Alvaro pause. Then, advancing to the very brink of the precipice, as if to fill himself with emotions of awe at the might and grandeur around him, and crowd out all other feelings and thoughts, he stood in silence, suffered a recoil of his anger, jealousy, and disgust with himself at the result of his encounter with Zomara, and soon was hurried away, thought and feeling, in the old accustomed channel of philosophic contemplation and poetic fancy, that sank the individual and thrust up in bold relief external objects of his wonder, delight and comprehension. Striking to him was the phosphorescent sheen of the foam capping the waves, with diminished lustre far out on the sea, and fringing the rugged shore with fold upon fold of pearly, lustrous, faintly sparkling lace of light; and the wonder of this being the effect of an infinity of luminous animalcules impressed itself upon him with a distinctness never before experienced. Then came a revolution of the phenomenon in his mind, when, with kaleidoscopic variety, its phases were presented in turn, then combined with other facts or fancies, till parallels were considered, and finally a result determined, the effect of his knowledge, fancy, reflection and application combined—

Within this book the universe is planned,
Read it, if ye the whole would'st understand!—
Cried out the boastful Spirit of the Age
Unto the hoary-headed Hindoo Sage.

SAGE.
From this bold crag, what seest thou in the ocean?

SPIRIT.
I see naught but the waves in wild commotion,
Their ragged, upreared crests snow-white and bright
With a strange, lustrous, phosphorescent light.

15

Look up, now, into the great vault of heaven !—

I see the stars, the Crown, the Polar Seven,
The Pleiades, and that broad land of light,
The Milky Way, across the brow of night.

Presumptuous man, and would'st thou bid me look
Within the narrow compass of thy book,
To know the universe, its moving cause,
Its ultimate design and governing laws ;

When, 'twixt a mite and world, thy piercing eye
The smallest difference cannot descry ;
When to thy keen, discriminating sight,
In myriads, they both appear as light !

Go, take a drop of ocean's sparkling brine,
And make its hidden secrets wholly thine,
And thou hast, of the universal plan,
Learned more than ever yet has vain, vain man.

The universe, sum of Unknown and Known ;
Study the "individual" alone ;
The Known Finite will tell whenever writ
All knowledge of the Unknown Infinite.

Alvaro, now impressed with the futility of man's study and reason to comprehend the universe, when his faculties are so weak and erring as to regard an infinity of worlds and an infinity of mites under the one vague effect of light, was turned to contemplation of himself and his situation, which, after a few minutes, resolved itself into this train of thought, and which, coupled with the above, gives a clear idea of the inmost character of this deep, daring, and dangerous man, despite the doubt he so severely condemned.—This, the reward of study—of years of labor over tomes of learning—of years of racking thought to understand this world, and act thence in accordance with its laws,—this, the reward, to be, as it were, the fickle wind ! Aye, now I blow me like the gentle breeze that would hesitate even to rob the thistle of its down, or steal the perfume of the violet ; anon, I bluster like a whirling gust, that threatens to uproot an oak and raises only dust ; again, I knit my brows, and with a sullen howl, hang round these ocean cliffs even like the storm to-

night ; again, I rage and roar, blind passion's hurricane, that would hurl down the castle of my father over his hoary head, and bury him—my sacred sire, and even myself beneath the ruins : uncertain, rash and ruthless wind !—Curse on the years of study that have borne, not Wisdom, fair and good, but Doubt, the monster, foul and grim ! Do I love Isabel ? Ten hours ago, I could have sworn I did ; nine hours ago my tongue was dumb ; eight hours ago, I could have thrown me at her feet in worship, and dared a crusade for her holy shrine ; an hour from then my arm was palsied, and my sword made blunt, while my harmless tongue did vaunt it like a turkey-cock ! —This damning doubt in action !—The saucy upstart, traitor to his king, and traitor to his friend, to cross my pathway at the very gate of Heaven, and I stand by, with humbled head and bended knee, to let him enter !

With this personal taunt, Alvaro was about to retire from the cliff, where his reflections found such a free scope, but to his great chagrin and disgust, when, as the moon gleamed suddenly through a broken cloud, he saw Zomara at the base of the cliff, about to essay its ascent !

Aha,—thought he,—more treachery, and at the dead of night ! Aye, and what time and place more fitting for my revenge ! I'll stab the villain as he gains the summit out of breath—let the cover of night conceal the deed—and the waves below forever bury the dead ! O God, if ever I believed in Thee and Thy justice, and vengeance to offending man, it is now !—But, hold—Alvaro guilty of cowardice? and crime attendant thereto? and have remorse gnaw till ruin of self and soul would be the only relief ? No, no ; with all that is damning in my composition, I'll not add cowardice ! And Zomara, traitor though he be to the crown, and rival though he be to obtain the greatest prize on earth, yet he is a brave, frank soldier, and I'll match him with courage, if not with might and skill !

So concluding, he withdrew a short distance toward Altanero's mansion, and stood behind a ledge, where, unobserved, he could await the coming of Zomara, ascertain his object, and act hence as he might deem best. And scarcely had he concealed himself, when, the moon bursting forth with a clear flood of light, two female figures were observed approaching, and were now not more than thirty paces distant, and, at the first glance, he recognized Isabel and Teresa!

VII.

GROW faint, Teresa.

'Tis the storm that appals you—the wild war of the elements around you—the time—the occasion—Zomara!

Alas! no; it is the stealth with which I creep from the house of love and care and safety, of those most dear to me, into the bleak, stormy night of uncertainty, mayhap, bliss—mayhap, misery!

And the frame, my lady, be it man or woman, that balances happiness in one hand and woe in the other, wavers for aye; for that balance is never adjusted! But faint not; for the moment approaches when delight will fall so heavily in one scale, and the rebound will be so rapid to the side of woe, that the balance will be shattered before recovery from the shock is gained.

Does it not grow late, Teresa? The time must surely have flown.

No, my lady; time lags for the eager and expectant, if it be only to buffet and baffle the spirit till the price is paid.

Alas! Teresa, I am sinking. Zomara is not here. He cannot live in the surf that lashes the rocks below, with such a deafening roar! Alas! I have led him to his death!

No! no! beloved one!—exclaimed Zomara, gaining the level of the cliff, and taking the fainting form of Isabel in his arms;—say, rather to life, the acme of living, to love!

Yes, embrace,—thought Teresa, as she stepped back a few paces, that their expression of feeling and thought might be without that chilling restraint—that distressing, harrassing restraint of the presence of a third person, be it the nearest and the dearest friend, when, in the first flutterings of love, heads and hearts find themselves in sudden communion, and confusion comes as certain as fate.—Yes, embrace,—thought Teresa,—and to your hearts' full measure of content. Does not Dame Nature wink in twilight, and close her eyes in utter darkness, at love's delight? Then why should I, who once did feel the mystic charm and know its ecstacy, more heed the act than she, whose mimic bauble plaything I have been, and all must be?

Dear Isabel,—at length said Zomara to the object of his affection, as he felt her fainting spirits revive and her bosom swell with the emotions of love, till her heart beat full and quick, and diffused its vigor through her glowing blood, till, responsive to the faintest whisper, and the gentlest pressure, she stood the very embodiment of love itself,—Dear Isabel, my life pays the forfeit, if I be found within this realm before two years expire—so runs my monarch's decree. Even now my conscience warns me that, for my foothold on this barren cliff, the price is death. But love has waived aside the honor nothing else could move—the bribe to hold you in my arms once more, breaks down the pride that bids me hence.

Once more! Alas! the cruel reminder your words betray. Once more! It sounds like a knell to which my heart gives audible response. Once more to hold me in your arms?

Say, then, forever?

Forever, let it be. The vow out-spoken one year ago, when love was young and timid, will not halt now at maturity, however great the courage the occasion demands.

Brave woman! noble in your inmost nature! Had Spain a thousand of your heroic blood, she would soon sway the world!

Alas! no, Zomara; I tremble even now at the expressions my hasty impulse conjured up. Weak and timid woman, call me rather—an uncertain semblance between a pallor and a flush—a wavering pendulum between hope and despair.

Ha! my love, the mirror of self is always warped. Nor man nor woman sees but a distorted image in this glass. You did not swoon away to-day at the clash of swords and the shedding of blood in deadly strife; you did not shrink from the storm to-night, which, though broken several hours ago, is yet wild and terrible on this jutting rock.

It was love, Zomara, not the woman, that braved and dared all this.

Then which will I embrace, love or the woman, for this heroism? Quick, ere your logic undoes you!

Both—both! Inseparably united, they are one. But jest no more, Zomara.

Not jest? Why, my love, my heart is bounding light and free, and feels responsive to its every throb a sympathetic mate; and not jest in such a happy mood with the fair lady that takes issue with that sympathetic heart?

No, Zomara; jest with a woman, but not with a woman united with love; for the former is but a playful flash, and the latter a flame aglow, feeding itself with its own light, till the whole body is illumined, and flickers not till the two are separated, and the flame extinguished—mayhap, with a jest.

True, Isabel; but a soldier jests with his life, holds his head upon his shoulders as a bauble—

No, Zomara; else woe to Isabel, who unites herself and soul with that which is held in such slight estimation.

True, Isabel; I yield submissive, and forgiveness crave. I do prize my life, for it is indissoluble with another that makes earth a paradise; and as my soul yearns for immortal bliss, I cannot lightly hold at heart this antepast.—Aglow again! pure, confiding, faithful heart. Now away with logic and jests giving wings to time, when every moment is a jewel in the diadem of life. And startle not—too many moments have already sped in idle words—our stay here must be brief.

Oh, go not yet, Zomara; talk not of it; but breathe to me your hopes—your aim—your destination—and your quick return.

In brief, then, Isabel, I came to take you hence to-night, far from the grief and torture of your love delayed, from the suit and sight of Alvaro spurned, and from the anger of your thwarted father.

Alas! the extremity!—But where, Zomara, could we escape all these?

In Cyprus, my love. Thither I go, an exile from Spain; but with you I go with a world in my arms instead.

In Cyprus!

Yes, in Cyprus; where await the softest nest for fleeing birds, the gentlest winds to kiss the cheek, the rarest flowers to charm the eye, and spread around their rich perfumes, the sweetest music from the warbling of the birds, and sighing of the winds, and fruits and vines that proudly might have hung in Eden's bowers,—all these await our happy bridal hour in Cyprus' isle, love-decked of old by Venus herself. There, will you go with me, dear Isabel?

Zomara, ask me not. My parents grow to age, and need that care which love, a daughter's love, alone bestows. Can you not turn aside the wrath of our good king, return to Spain, and win your way to my father's heart, as you have done to mine?

No, Isabel, there's nothing but free and prompt obedience that will prevail against our king's displeasure, once incurred. Were this not so, your father never would hear my name, unless to launch fresh curses at my head. But fly with me, a loving, trusting bride, and when two years have passed in joy in our bright island home, we will return to Spain with honor and with pride; the king once more will smile on Zomara; wealth and station come again to him, and these may win him smiles where there is now no favor. Dear Isabel, no hope is left to us, save that which sails my waiting ship with you, most precious freight on board. If you remain, I go, with constant sorrow and despair, most fit companions for a lonely exile, to wander, and ere long to die. Yes, death would be relief to life which held not you.

No more. The royal ban, which drives you hence, expels me, too, for we are one. Where you are, I must be.—Teresa!—One moment—then—

And Isabel, joining Teresa to divulge the awful secret of her flight to her confidante and adviser, secure her co-operation and assistance in getting ready a few necessary articles of dress, stole back to her father's house, and disappeared in the darkness of the vineyard and grove of pomegranates near the veranda.

VIII.

AT this opportune moment for revenge, what Spaniard could remain unmoved with but a drop of the haughty blood that boiled in the veins of Alvaro, as he witnessed the interview between Zomara and Isabel and divined its purport, if he heard not all their conversation? So, with hurried step, and haughty strut, as if the very earth should tremble beneath his tread, he advanced within a few paces of Zomara, and sternly said, but with a bitterness and assumed derision that betrayed the galling he had been but recently subjected to—

Zomara of Castile, your sword. Your life is now your king's. Yield, sir, or perish by the avenging sword of him whose dearest plans you dare to thwart—most thankful that the baser blade of a common executioner, or a hireling, for the reward offered for the head of a traitor, sends not your spirit to eternity!

Approach me not, Alvaro,—as sternly spoke Zomara, but with a coolness and complacency that was most taunting to his hasty rival,—approach me not, or, by our Holy Faith, this sword, never stained but with the blood of the enemies of Spain until to-day, shall wash away its gory honors in the foul life-blood of a base and treacherous spy— a bandit, in the guise of a nobleman.

And, as happened scarcely twelve hours before, these onetime bosom friends and constant companions were, in another instant, in deadly combat, the clangor of their Toledos trusty ringing out clear above the roar of the waves, the rumble of distant thunder, and the wail of the winds. And Teresa, hearing faintly the voices of the combatants as she, following Isabel, was about to enter the house, paused, heard the clash of the swords, surmised the affray correctly, left Isabel abruptly, and stole back to the cliff; and, from the very place Alvaro had observed the interview, witnessed, in dire dismay and abject terror, the progress of the combat. Isabel, however, missing Teresa

from her side, and her timidity and terror at her unexpected desertion almost overpowering her, turned, too, from the house into the garden, and, hearing the din of clashing steel, with trembling and uncertain steps hastened again to the brow of the cliff. At the very moment, too, that she approached in sight, Zomara, tripping over a little ledge in the uneven surface, received a powerful blow, which, though parried near the hilt, having lost his balance, sent him staggering backward, directly across the path of Isabel, over the cliff into the sea!

Isabel saw that it was Zomara—no more—her eyes so riveted on him as he staggered before her, that they almost carried her over the cliff in the intensity of her eagerness to behold his fate. With a faint shriek, followed by a fainter exclamation— O God! it is he!—she sank insensible to the ground.

Yes! O God! it is he!—repeated Teresa, as her eyes, as intently fixed on Alvaro as Isabel's were on Zomara, followed him, as he retreated rapidly, awe-struck at the unexpected termination of the duel, and feeling in an instant his guilt and the dread of discovery; for the din must have alarmed at least the ladies, who had but a few minutes before withdrawn from the scene of the affray.—Yes, it is he!—applying the phrase to Alvaro, who, in her very presence, but unknown to him, had committed the most heinous crime of murder; for, toppled from the cliff into the raging sea beneath, was death so certainly in her opinion, it was not questioned, but admitted as a damning fact on the instant.

Alvaro! Alvaro!—she exclaimed, from the depth of her anguish,—was it not enough to blight a loving girl's confiding heart, to separate the mother from her babe, and drive her forth into a cold, unpitying world, with nothing to hide her loathsome leprosy but this poor, flimsy garment of a governess, which keen suspicion's first and faintest word would cut away, but must you burden her still more with the sight of your foul murder of a fellow-man? Woe! woe! to love a base betrayer! Woe! woe! to love a murderer! Woe! woe! to bear the constant, pointed pain and crushing burden of his guilt—a loved one's guilt—and all alone!

And with this revelation, wrung from the soul-harrowed woman in a moment of almost suicidal misery and despair, you gain the key of her hidden history, which will unlock to your clear comprehension her actions in the future.

Help! help! a light!—cried out Isabel, recovering from her swoon, and awakening, as it were, from a horrible nightmare. Then, clinging and appealing to Teresa.—Is this the night, Teresa? Was it the spectre of a dream? Or, did I see Zomara, wounded, fall into the sea? Oh, say, Teresa, it was the spectre of a dream!

And Teresa, catching the idea of the spectre of a dream, with that brooding philosophy and melancholy combined that characterized this deeply feeling and thinking woman, weirdly extended it and its accompaniments to human life.—It was the spectre of the dream of life—the night which ends in death! And more than thou are dreaming of the spectres of fell murder,—more than thou are blindly staring in this night whose morn is in the grave! Rise, Isabel, for more than thou are bending under woes whose weight exceeds thine own. Poor child, it is the night, but thou, though staring in thy sleep, canst not perceive the gloom. Thy sad awakening is near at hand, and then—thy dream of love is over!

IX.

BUT what means this excitement in the mansion of the Altaneros—this hurrying and rushing to and fro—this calling for Martin, and Pedro, and Nona—this carrying of lights in every direction—this lamentation of Altanero—this swearing of old Borracho?—for the old Don, discussing the exciting events of the day, had not been allowed to go home at his usual time, but must remain for the night. You might imagine what all this excitement and confusion is about. It was discovered that Isabel and Teresa had disappeared! and conjecture and surmise were not long in determining an elopement with the daring, dashing young soldier, who had fallen like a firebrand in their midst, and set them all ablaze. And here comes Altanero, bemoaning his supposed loss, and suspicious that she has descended the rugged natural steps of the cliff in the garden, and dared the stormy waters with her lover, to share his exile, rather than endure his absence and her parent's anger; and Lady Mariana, and Borracho, and attendants, follow like a rabble, not exactly knowing why, but because Altanero is in the lead.

O Isabel!—bemoaned the distracted father,—that you should prove so ungrateful—that you should desert your aged father—disgrace and desolate the home your presence made so happy! My daughter, O my daughter, come back!—O angry sea, spare her life! O storm-king, drive her back to me—the erring girl, she knows not what she does!

Call not, blind father, on the sea and storm,—said Teresa, calmly.—Restrain your clamorous grief. Your daughter is here.

My child, my child! O Heavenly Father, I thank Thee!—exclaimed Lady Mariana, sinking on her knees, and offering up a grateful prayer.

Aha!—cried out the impulsive Borracho,—I told you she had not fled.

Because she could not,—added solemn Pedro, half aloud to Nona, clinging to him in the darkness and excitement, and half concealed within himself in confirmation of his philosophic belief,—a woman's a woman the wide world over.

But Altanero, unheeding everything else, and filled with the most affectionate feelings of a fond father for an only and beloved child, stooped over Isabel, kissed her forehead tenderly, and raised her gently from the ground. There was a self accusation in him, too, that found relief in the discovery of Isabel. It was greatly owing to himself, the unhappy events of the day before, and he would willingly make amends. Hence to his daughter a greater demonstration of his affection, which was genuine, was a natural result.—You have not fled from me, Isabel,—he said, but in a tone that rather blamed himself for the thought, than accused her of the attempt.—Oh, joy to hold you in my arms again,—embracing her fondly, but in a manner seemingly selfish, as if to exclude the rest of the world from sharing such happiness.—Look up and speak to me, dear daughter.

There was deep silence after this expression of love in action and word. Even Borracho, who was about to utter his thought on the moment,—for he was too much the creature of impulse to act from reflection and memory,—hesitated; and the lull that followed was almost breathless. But before Isabel, preparatory to addressing her father, could raise her head, and turn her countenance toward him, the company were chilled to the marrow with a cry of distress, that rose above the surge of the sea, and pierced the ear, and sank into the soul of every one whereon the impress of Heaven was at all traceable—

Help! help!

'Tis he! 'tis Zomara, father!—exclaimed Isabel, starting up wildly.—'Tis Zomara, father—dear father, save him! Wounded, and hurled from the cliff, he struggles in the waves below! He cries for help! O father, save him! save him! and save your daughter, too!—with that wonderful faculty that woman possesses of bringing to bear all her resources in an instant, Isabel, at this awful moment, did not fail to lay stress on an appeal to the affection demonstrated but a few minutes before; and the appeal was not without its effect.

My daughter, yes,—answered Altanero, in gentle but determined tones,—a traitor to the king he may be, and a stab in my very heart, as he is, yet no human being ever called for help in Altanero's ear in vain. Martin! a rope!

And almost at the same instant, Borracho had determined on a rescue, too. Wounded and hurled from the cliff? By whom? By his own son!—a conclusion he must, and did come to, from the premises, though he knew nothing more than the events of the past day. He must be saved, or Alvaro is a murderer!

Get a rope, Pedro! a rope,—cried out Borracho, taking the cue from Altanero, who had several times previously lowered a man from above to assist or save persons in distress below.—Though it tears my soul to shreds,—he added, inwardly,—this must be the rash work of my son!

A rope?—drawled out Pedro.

A rope? yes; you snailed-faced dullard. And quick! or, once suspended over this cliff, you'll dangle there till doomsday, if for nothing else than a gull-scare!

But Martin, already sobered, and restored to his accustomed activity of mind and body, had already returned from the house with a rope. And having formed a loop or noose with it as he ran, he threw the same over Pedro the instant he came up; and before Pedro seemed to be more than half conscious of the act, he was over the brink going down the declivity that was almost precipitous in a way that seemed more likely to knock his seven senses about his ears, than to steady them in their little chamber in his skull. It was Martin's time now to get even with Pedro, and he availed himself of the opportunity—a piece of strategy that Nona, ostensibly very anxious about the safety of Pedro over the cliff, did not fail to observe; for what woman so blind that she cannot, from her centre of observation, see the workings and windings of rivalry and jealousy around her; and, as Pedro would like to be able to say at this moment, and apply to Nona, a woman's a woman the wide world over! Yes; Nona not only observed this little manœuvre of Martin, but actually, and during the height of the excitement, did express her approval of the same by nudging Martin very significantly under the ribs, as she essayed to assist him in keeping poor Pedro, in a double sense, in suspense!

But however amusing and humorous this episode, it was so by contrast with the occasion, a moment of the most agonizing excitement and suspense to all others on the rock—comedy only by contrast with tragedy in a most terrible form.

Borracho, standing on the brink and waiving a torch, was calling out to Pedro—No quaking now! Hold fast with one hand to the rope, to steady yourself, and with the other cling to the rocks, lest you go too fast! Run along the narrow beach as far as the rope will allow you! Save this soldier's life, and you have more of which to boast than he with all his blood-purchased honors!—and more such directions in detail and comments on the act, as were as little heard as heeded, if they had been heard.

Altanero stood by Isabel; his head drooping on his bosom, as he beheld the agony of his beloved daughter, and heard her plaintive moan. And when she kneeled, and clasped her hands, breathing a prayer to Heaven to save the life of Zomara, he sank by her side with involuntary sympathy, and repeated her prayer in spirit, if not in voice.

O Holy Mother,—said Isabel, in tones that asserted the dictation of her soul,—whose Son didst still the angry billows, and walk the humbled waves of Galilee, implore with Him for Zomara's life! Save him! O Holy Mother, save him!

Amen!

And Teresa, wrought to the same pitch as Isabel, but not forgetting the relationship in which she stood, and was known only to herself, turned her face away from the glaring torch, lest its light would reveal the secret of her misery, and breathed as earnest and fervid a prayer to the Most High as her entirety of feeling and thought could concentrate to—O God of pity, give this brave man the strength to save the life of Zomara, and spare Alvaro's brow, already scorched, from the damning brand of murder!—A prayer to which Borracho, had he heard it, would have cried aloud, most fervently—Amen! But little he dreamed he had by his side a companion, in his interest for Zomara, not so much for Zomara's sake, but Alvaro's!

But during this period, perhaps as long as the time I have taken in narrating the circumstances, Pedro, reached the narrow beach; and almost immediately afterward, he found a man clinging like a limpet to a rock, the waves, every now and then, washing almost entirely over the poor fellow's body. With more alertness and adroitness, than might be supposed, the droll, drawling, philosophic semblance of a man was capable of, Pedro forthwith lashed the man to himself with the rope's end, hallooed and shouted to those above to pull away, and jerked at the dangling rope till he was assured by its increasing tension that his signal was understood, and then began the ascent with his heavy burden. It was a difficult as it was a dangerous task. Every foothold had to be sought, and cautiously tested before trusting it

with the full weight of himself and burden; so every crag or prominence was tried, that he clung to with his right hand, for his left arm encircled the rescued man; but receiving steadiness from the tautness of the rope, and great assistance from the pulling above of Borracho, Altanero, Martin, and Nona, the ascent was possible, and accomplished in really a short time, however painfully long it appeared to everybody.

Oh, what a sigh of relief and prayer of thanks went up as Pedro reached the top, and laid his burden on the ground beside which he was almost ready himself to sink from exhaustion!

A thousand pistoles for this act, Pedro!—exclaimed Borracho, as he dropped the rope and hurried to pick up from the ground his torch, thrown down in his eagerness to assist at the rope, and almost extinguished now for the lack of air.

But as the light of the rekindling torch lit up the outlines, and at length the features of the rescued man, a shudder seized Borracho, nearest to him, that seemed to concentrate about his heart and freeze it to the core!—IT IS NOT ZOMARA!—he said, in scarcely an audible tone, and yet it hushed the howl of the storm, and the roar of the sea, and left the earth suspended in silence, before it was barely uttered!

Not Zomara!—faintly echoed Isabel, who, about to stoop and embrace the rescued man, recoiled, and sank into the arms of her father, breathing, with her last breath of sensibility, that one word Farewell!—so ominous, so often, that it ever sounds like the echo of a footfall in that weird old castle whose portal is the grave!

Not Zomara!—sighed Teresa, turning into the darkness, as more fitting for her silent communion with despair.—Not Zomara! Then he is dead! and Alvaro is a murderer! and woe! woe! the awful secret is mine alone! for, save the all-seeing God, Teresa was the only witness to his crime!

Well, if not Zomara, who was the rescued man? An answer to this pertinent question he gave himself, in a few minutes after he was landed on the cliff. Raising his body from the ground, and resting on one arm, and in that significant and impressive posture, immortalized in the Dying

Gladiator, he told his story briefly—My thanks, good sirs, for aid. But it came too late. The hope of the pirate, the dread of the sea, lies wrecked on the rocks below! and I will not long survive her fate! A leak, good sirs; a run into the harbor, however dangerous in such a sou'wester; a crash! and the vessel parted, and seventy pirates, as daring and dreaded as ever nailed a black flag to the mast, were floundering in the sea! But we go together—the Black Eagle and her commander! Aye! aye! and there's comfort in death, in robbing the gallows! But I thank you, good sirs, for aid, though too—

Late! too late!—added Borracho, finishing the sentence of the pirate, broken off by death; for, however disappointed in not rescuing Zomara, his feelings were aroused by the expressions and tone of the dying pirate, and he felt he would have been happy if he had saved the life of a wretch boastful of his criminal life even with his dying breath.

It is possible that another attempt would have been made to rescue Zomara, had Isabel recovered from her swoon; but, exhausted and worn out by the excitement of the past day and night, the frequent transitions from the heights of happiness to the depths of despair, she lay so like death, that she was borne to her chamber before she recovered consciousness; and this was of short duration, for she lapsed almost immediately afterward into delirium, from which, and the fever accompanying, she did not recover for a fortnight.

Teresa was satisfied he was dead; so was Altanero; so was Borracho; and in the interest taken in Isabel, and under the unfavorable circumstances for prosecuting the search till daybreak at least, it is not surprising that a second effort was not made. It was conjectured, moreover, that the Zomara that Isabel saw fall over the cliff was but the vision of an excited imagination—a conjecture that Teresa confirmed by referring to what she saw as a spectre—a spectre in the dream of life—a conjecture that was so satisfying that nobody was at all anxious to distrust it, or scrutinize it too closely. The report ran through the town the next morning, moreover, that a pirate's vessel had been wrecked, and several of the pirates rescued, but nothing was heard of Zomara, and while his death was accepted by Isabel, Teresa, and Alvaro, and his absence was all that the others desired, his whereabouts were no longer cared about or inquired for.

X.

ZOMARA was dead, as far as the principal characters of this story were concerned, and we will consider him so, till time and circumstances restore him to life, to take a leading part in this drama of life. And though the thread of the narrative here parts into two strands, one pertaining to Isabel, the other to Zomara, the former is so much the more like a continuance than the latter, that it must be followed for a while at least, and the other dropped.

Poor Isabel! for a fortnight after the terrible scenes already described, she lay sick with a brain fever. Soon after she was carried to her room, she was seized with a chill, which culminated in a slight convulsion. An intense head-ache racked her brain. Her skin grew hot and dry, and her pulse hard and rapid. Her face alternately flushed and turned pallid; and her eyes, so soft, so mild, and retiring in health, now stared wildly about through a suffusion of tears. Her senses, too, of sight and hearing were perverted, and made painfully sensitive to light and sound. Sleep and rest and happy dreams were banished from her pillow, and in their stead were eager watchfulness, restlessness, with frequent twitchings of her delicately-wrought muscles, and delirium—that madness of the mind so heartrending in a beloved one—that calls on the attendant for answers to the most varied of questions, trivial, grave, pertinent, remote, sad and severe; that bids you listen to imagined sounds, the softest strains of music, the startling cry of fire, the whisper of love, the rattle of musketry, the sighing of the zephyr, and the roar of the storm; and that directs the mournful eye to illusive sights, a basket of roses scattered on the counterpane, the face of an absent friend, a token of love, a spectre, a dagger dripping with blood, Zomara falling into the sea.

The most celebrated physician in Grenada was dispatched for, and, after several hours of intense anxiety and impatience, during which time the doctor finished his forty winks after the first bell, rose, dressed himself at his leisure, breakfasted without any danger of incurring dyspepsia from hurried and imperfect mastication, straddled a pair of saddle-bags thrown across a snail-paced donkey, at length arrived at Altanero's door, and was ushered into the chamber of Isabel.

No; Dr. Quesada was not another Sangrado; nor was he an ignorant pretender, a charlatan, or, in the phrase of the day, a quack; but a gentleman learned in the lore of his profession: kind-hearted and courteous, but lapsing latterly, as he grew old, into laziness and a regular routine practice—a business to gain his livelihood that awakened little sympathy or philanthropic feeling in him for his patients. As he grew old, moreover, he became technical, not only with the terms of his profession, but with its ethics, synonymous with exclusiveness, dignity, and pride; and, in his wide and varied practice, he brooked neither disagreement nor contradiction, but exhibited irritability and impatience on the slightest provocation. However, not to weary you with detailed descriptions, I will hasten on to a scene that followed the doctor's retiring from the sick chamber, that not only exhibits the character of the physician, but marks a step in the progress of the story.

Altanero had followed, with noiseless tread, after Dr. Quesada into the chamber, had watched his every motion and expression, to detect his inmost thought, and now sought, on his withdrawing into the hall, to relieve his baffled intent and eagerness in words, for he failed to determine anything from the physician's routine actions. And Quesada was about to reply in his usual way, when he was interrupted by the arrival of Alvaro.

Alvaro was not only anxious to know if he was suspected of the murder of Zomara; or, if—worse a thousand fold over—he had been seen by anybody in the commission of the heinous crime; he was anxious, too, about the fate of Isabel, for rumor, through the mouth of Nona, had whispered in his ear that she was a raving maniac; and come now the very worst, as the result of his rash act, he was daring enough to meet it face to face, determined to allay suspicion at once by his unmoved presence, deny or disprove the assertions of witnesses with his unhesitating speech and subtle argument; and, possibly, relieve Isabel, if raving, as reported, by means of his knowledge; for the art of the physician had not been ignored by him in his greed to gorge his maw with worldly wisdom, but it was made a special study, that yielded him the most stable rocks, whereon to build the structure of his philosophy; and though he practiced not the art, his princely fortune and estates preventing, if not his desire, yet to stay the sad havoc of his crime, and save the woman for whom he had staked, and, perhaps lost, the salvation of his soul, he was courageous enough to dare the attempt.

By your leave, Don Altanero,—said Alvaro,—I would ask this most learned physician—

What my diagnosis is?—said Quesada, breaking in, and finishing the sentence, as he supposed, in the most technical, unintelligible, and pretentious manner.

My son,—said Altanero, kindly, and determined to show his appreciation of Alvaro's interest in his daughter, as well to express a renewal of his hope that his plans would be consummated, now that Zomara was gone, dead or in exile, it mattered little which,—my son, I thank you, you may, though I was about to ask him what was the malady of my daughter.

My lord,—said Alvaro, perceiving Altanero's ignorance of Quesada's speech,—his answer to my question will be an answer to yours. Your diagnosis, if you please, good doctor?

There was an earnestness and directness about the question of Alvaro, that made Quesada hesitate, as it also slightly ruffled his temper.

An inflammation, -ir, an—stammered the doctor, his confusion resulting from the unlooked for question so direct.

An inflammation! So general, most learned physician, I would take your word as synonymous with ablaze—the patient, as it were, aflame with passion, love, hate, anger, jealousy, as the case might be. Be more specific, if you please.

What! my lord, turned inquisitor?—said Quesada, concealing his rising anger under satire.

As you like it,—replied Alvaro, on the instant comprehending the physician's thrust,—and with a conscience that constructs a rack for the mute and obstinate.

Well, my lord, since you are so persistent and determined,—said the disciple of Æsculapius, rising at least an inch higher and expanding proportionately, as his haughtiness was fully aroused,—I pronounce this a case of inflammation of the pia mater and arachnoid—

The meninges, most learned doctor; and meningitis your diagnosis. The symptoms, what, upon which you base this opinion?

Intolerable! my lord,—exclaimed Quesada, offended and astonished, with a little suspicion and fear just entering its wedge-point into his understanding.

By your leave, my lord Altanero,—said Alvaro, turning abruptly from Quesada,—I will acquaint myself with the symptoms, and lest my presence excite your beloved daughter, I will steal into her chamber on tiptoe, unseen and unheard by her, if she have the eyes and ears of Heimdall himself.

My son,—replied Altanero,—your interest and anxiety for my poor daughter are not misunderstood. Go; and thanks, kind-hearted son,—emphasizing the word son, that the offended Quesada might infer the new relationship that was projected between the two most noble families in the town.

No, my lord,—said Quesada, stepping sternly in front of the door, and barricading it with his person.—No, my lord; nor king nor courtier crosses the threshold of the sick-chamber without a permit from the physician; for in the narrow compass of these walls his fiat is supreme above all worldly power.

What! cross my path and stand between me and that which is nearest and dearest to my soul! Aside, most learned doctor,—said Alvaro, excitedly, waiving the physician to one side.

Not for my life!—exclaimed Quesada, whipping out a lancet, with a great show of courage.—With this little blade, no longer than my lady's thumb nail, I defy the longest sword in Spain!

You do, most valiant doctor?—said Alvaro, with a sneer; and, drawing his sword, he pricked him with a series of mock thrusts in rapid succession, till thoroughly frightened, and feeling outraged and humiliated to the core, the pompous old doctor danced backward in the most ludicrous manner, brandishing his lancet the while, and even crying murder, till Alvaro desisted, with another sneer of contempt, and passed, without hindrance, into an anteroom, whence, when an opportune moment arrived, unperceived by Isabel, he stole into her chamber to the back of the couch, on which she tossed in the excitement and delirium of her disease.

With what keen and agonizing intensity his eye pierced through each symptom as a result to ascertain the cause! And when he became conscious that the malady had not been exaggerated by either Nona or Quesada, though he might differ in his diagnosis slightly with the latter, a sense of his guilt, and its extending terrible effects, became so oppressive to him that he immediately withdrew, but not so cautiously as he entered,—for the sensitive ear of Isabel caught the sound of his retreating steps. With a wild gleam in her eye, she raised her head from the pillow, caught a sight of Alvaro, but whether or not she recognized him, with her perverted vision, cannot be said, and cried aloud—

Do not leave me, Alvaro! You did not commit the deed! Your eyes are not on fire, and your hand is not red with blood! Oh, do not fly from me, Alvaro! Friend of my childhood, noble Alvaro, it was not for you to drive the fiery dagger in my brow that is searing my brain!

But Alvaro did fly from her. Guilt may brave accusations and condemnations without number; but held up as angelic purity to be worshiped, it must quail in an instant.

Teresa, on her knees by the side of the couch, her face buried between her hands bathed in tears, and now almost worn out with watching, did not observe Alvaro in the room; but when she heard his name mentioned, and in connection with innocence, she started as if she heard a revocation of his crimes from the Most High. But, alas! the source of delirium asserted itself to the contrary, when she saw the glaring eye of Isabel, and beheld her ghastly countenance! Rising sorrowfully, accordingly, she gently pressed the excited Isabel back on her pillow, composed her tenderly, with that touch that belongs only to a woman, and a woman that has suffered, then sank again on her knees, and bowed her head.

XI.

QUESADA foamed and raged through the hall until Alvaro came out of the chamber. He had never in his life been so grossly insulted. He pronounced Alvaro a maniac. No man in his senses would have acted in such an outrageous manner to him, the most celebrated physician in Grenada, and so rashly with respect to Isabel.

A maniac, Don Altanero, as sure as the world!

I grant you he is hot and hasty, rash in the extreme; but not insane. He is too profound a philosopher to be insane.

Ah, there you mistake. The impetuosity of his great mind once aroused, oversteps the bounds of reason, runs wild, and in such an extraordinary way, I am in amaze! I would like to bleed him, I would! This little instrument would restore his rashness to reason, sooner than any other remedy in the pharmacopoeia. Bleed him? I'd bleed him till he'd faint; there would be no more of this rashness after that!

Your pardon most humbly I crave, most worthy doctor,—said Alvaro, approaching the truculent Quesada in a mild and submissive manner.—Your diagnosis is correct enough—

Mania, as well marked as ever I witnessed in my life!—roared Quesada.

Meningitis, you said but a moment ago.

Madness, unmistakably!—cried Quesada.

No, most learned doctor; you go too far. The inflammation may have extended to the tunics of the brain, as you supposed; but I think the cerebral substance is alone involved,—witness the perverted senses of sight and hearing, the slight convulsions, the agitation of the limbs, and the well marked tremors, occurring on the one side. Cerebritis, say I.

Mania! acute mania! by all the books outside of Egypt!—still roared out Quesada.

'Tis true, most learned doctor, acute mania may result from sudden and great grief and violent shocks to the nervous system; and, alas! that I should be the unwilling cause of any such to Isabel. 'Tis true, moreover, there is delusion and—suddenly checking himself, as he reflected, that perhaps it were better far, that there was delusion; then continuing his argument,—but you ignore the fever, the convulsions, the intense headache,—

Insanity, my lord!—again exclaimed Quesada, to Don Altanero.—But, whispering to him,—such medical logic I never heard since I left the university. He astonishes me; but the insane do most extraordinary things.

'Tis true, too, learned Quesada,—continued Alvaro,—the intense brilliancy of the eye would lead you to suspect meningitis or insanity, but—

Hold! hold! Alvaro,—exclaimed Quesada,—your eye has not the great brilliancy of which you speak!

My eye! my eye! Your meaning, sir? Quibble with me again, will you?—Now for your treatment, what do you propose?

The lancet! bleed to syncope—relieve you of your mania more speedily than any other known remedy!

My mania! my mania! What, most valiant doctor, would you make a gibe of me on such an occasion like this? What mockery is this in your profession?

Restrain yourself, my son,—said Altanero, here interposing not only in speech but in person,—you misunderstand each other. My son, worthy Quesada, in his anger at your haste and apparent rudeness, calls you mad, not Isabel; and, learned Quesada, you must confess Alvaro talks not without reason. Understand one another. Be friends. Unite your wisdom and skill to relieve, perhaps, save my daughter, and the thanks and gratitude of an aged father bring blessings on you to the grave.

Your hand, most learned Quesada,—said Alvaro.

And the pompous old physician, and the rash young philosopher embraced as friends, and were friends henceforth. And by their united knowledge and skill, combined with the most tender and careful nursing by Lady Mariana and Teresa, in about two weeks time Isabel was so far recovered that Quesada retired, with the richest fee he ever pocketed in his practice, and she was left in the care of her family and Alvaro, her restoration assured.

XII.

HOWEVER, Isabel, her health assured, nay, regained, was not happy. Far from it. There was a sorrow stifling her heart, that forbade its expanding into mirth and gayety. Yet there was a sweetness about her sadness that bore the semblance of happiness; and as days passed by, and weeks and months were buried in the past, to all outward appearances she was reconciled to her fate—alone in a world of love! But, melancholy marked her as its own. In the silent brooding of her heart, the spirit of Zomara was ever in communion with her soul. His presence pervaded the atmosphere. She was sensible of it; but it was to her the presence of the dead, the loved and the lost.

Many a time and oft she discoursed with Teresa, and unbosomed to her her inmost thought and feeling. There was comfort in this. An emotion excited is like any other force, not relieved till expended. There was comfort to both in this; for Teresa's existence, too, was in that sub-stratum of silence and corroding sorrow, where sympathy is the nearest if not the only approach to joy.

But there were times when Isabel was alone, without this companion in sorrow and grief by her side; when Teresa, called away by household duties, or on her regular visits to some unknown place, nobody knew where, or cared to trace, she was as solitary in space as a single star in the heavens would be. And it was in one of these loneliest of periods, during the absence of Teresa from the town, on her unknown mission, that Isabel was sitting in the balcony of her chamber, gazing vacantly over the cliff where the scene that deadened her soul had transpired, and over the sea that buried beneath its glittering wave the form of him for whom her body was made and had its existence till sundered by the red hand of murder; and into the hazy heaven afar off, where the ocean and the sky joined and were lost in one another, so like—Ah, she had but one thought, one simile, and one that recurred at this particular moment with an intensity that exhibited itself in action, a startled look, a forward movement to the rail of the balcony on which she leaned, and a sigh; for that one simile was the union of Zomara and herself, soul and soul.

The sun sank beneath the wave. The fiery hand out-stretched across the ocean, as if to bid the lonely Isabel a fond good-night, disappeared in the glamour of its own gleam. Then began to glow the sky. And clouds that lay along the horizon, like sullen fog in a dismal valley, unfolded and developed into a world of beauty, with mountains of rose-petals pinnacled with gold, and seas of sapphire spangled with islands of diamond and pearl. Ah, there must be the haven of bliss—there love must live, where all is resplendent with beauty, and the calm and silence augur only of peace. Then faded the vision from sight, and a dull dusk crept stealthily over the face of heaven and earth. The bright dream vanished. The dusk of dismay was at hand.

But hark! the thrum of a guitar breaks the silence of the calm autumn eve, and awakens Isabel from her reverie. In an instant more a plaintive strain of melody reaches her appreciative ear, and she stoops to catch the singer's every word—

I saunter on the sandy shore,
    Where the waves seem'd merry girls,
Bedecking thems'lfs with seaweed and shells,
    And flowers of foam in their curls ;—
Where now I see in the foam a shroud,
    As if toss'd on eternity's bed,
And hear a moan from the depths unknown !—
    Alas ! he is dead ! he is dead !

I wander through the wooded glen,
    Where Nature seem'd a child,
That, 'round trees, play'd at catch, with
        the merry nut-hatch,
    And in the flow'rets smiled ;—
Where now the deadly night-shade grows,
    And the owl echoes, overhead,
The clods' mournful sound as they fell in
        the ground—
    Alas ! o'er the dead ! o'er the dead !

Ah ! there is no beauty again to the eye
    That bedews a lover's mould,
And no more music again to the ear
    That has heard a lover knoll'd ;
When the heart-strings are struck by the
        Harper of Death,
    Forever has harmony fled ;
The lark nevermore will with melody soar ;—
    Alas ! he is dead ! he is dead !

Alas ! he is dead !—sighed Isabel, as she withdrew from the balcony, and threw herself on her
couch, pressing her hands the while against her
eyes, as if to shut out the world from her contemplation and retirement. But the refrain of the
wandering minstrel's plaintive song rang in her
ears, and the spectre of Zomara, with all the distinctness of the apparition of Santiago, as he led
the Spaniards of old on to victory, glided before
her, stood like a statue, cold and unfeeling, and
gazed upon her with a sad and wondering eye ;
and, anon, pointed with a steady hand to the
casket containing the dagger, the only token in
material form she was possessed of from Zomara,
and in that posture vanished from sight, like a
mist dissolving in the gleam of a morning's sun.

How long the apparition of Zomara stood by
her side, or rather how long the hallucination had
possession of her mind, may be inferred from the
fact that when Isabel awoke the twilight had
gone, and night had come, and the glimmer of the
moon was faintly shining through the open win-

dows, casting a ghostly glamour about everything
in the room. Forthwith she arose, and, with
trembling steps, moved toward her dressing case,
laid her hand on the casket, opened it, and took
from thence Zomara's token, the dagger ! She
then moved toward a window, held the deadly
blade in the bright gleam of the moon-shine—held
it like a pretty plaything in her hand. Was life
becoming a bauble to her, too, that the instrument
of death should lie on her palm with no more terror than a toy ?

Mysterious token ! I marvel at thy meaning,—
thus ran her thoughts—a symbol of something
thou art, but, like the riddle of life and the riddle
of love, thy import is a blank. Nay ; there is but
one intent in a dagger, and that is death ! Death ?
to whom ? by whom ? Not Isabel by Zomara ?
That cannot be—he is dead. Then Isabel by Isabel ? Aye, though the shudder that seizes my soul
shatter it, this is thy terrible significance ! This
is the bridge that spans the awful chasm, sepa-
rating life from death, Isabel from Zomara. Is
there, then, but the length of a span, the length
of this gleaming blade, between me and my beloved ? How can I stay a minute longer ? I
come ! I come, Zomara !

And Isabel raised the dagger, turned its point
to her bosom, and uplifted her eyes to the Throne
of Grace, imploring, with a look of the most abject woe, forgiveness.

But deliberate self-murder ever halts. The
most timid doubt deters the dagger in its down-
ward course, dealing death. Isabel, determined on
destruction, with her last look on her hand to give
it the steadiness of her will, has her eyes fixed in an
instant, as if riveted by some mesmeric power, on
the hilt of the dagger, whereon she copies a heart !
She hesitates—she recoils ! The perspiration starts
from her pallid brow, and she sinks exhausted on
a chair by the window.

What signifies the heart ? Ah, who can doubt
it ? The life-throbbing organ, so responsive in its
action to the hopes and fears of love, when sym-
bolized, must mean love—the very essence of love !
Then here is the scallop, the badge of the pilgrim
to Santiago's holy shrine ; and, mark, it is nailed

to a cross, that holiest of holy emblems, testifying the crucifixion of the Son of God! Faith! faith eternal abides in these symbols. But what mockery and contradiction is this? Here gleams a blade, designed by man with one purpose only, and that is death! Ah, the riddle of the Sphinx is unsolved, and the forfeit, as of old, must be paid! But why sigh at the thought of death? Is not Zomara dead? And in that eternity beyond the grave, do not the dead commune? And do I dread communion with Zomara? with Zomara, for whom my soul yearns, and beats within the narrow walls of this frail frame to find an eyelet, such as this pretty bodkin could make in an instant, through which to join him in eternal bliss? Love, and faith in love, and faith in God, and death, to enjoy eternally —so reads the riddle!

And Isabel again rose to her feet, clutched the dagger with a firm grip, and directed a second time the point of the deadly instrument to her breast.

But the spectre of Zomara rose before her like a gleam of light! And in its hand it bore the semblance of the dagger with which she was about to

take her life. It held it on high, looked upon it with a satisfied and happy gaze, then pressed it thrice to its lips, and said, in solemn voice,—Love, trust in God, unto death—and disappeared as suddenly as it rose!

Isabel sank again into her chair, muttering aloud the reading of the riddle by the spectre,— Love, trust in God, unto death!

For, if you will recall her reasonings, you will observe that this interpretation of the apparition that rose before her disordered mind, is but one remove from her conclusions then expressed. The spectre was within, and not without her brain.

And as Isabel sank into the chair, Teresa returned, crossed the apartment, stood by her side, and added to poor Isabel's words,—

Yes, my lady; love the giver of that token with all your heart; trust with the faith that is typified by that holiest symbol of your religion; and be faithful until death!

Perceiving, then, with that seeming intuition that is the result of a sensitively sympathetic nature, that Isabel was under an undue and unhealthy excitement, she conducted her to her bed, subdued the activity of her mind, by gently stroking her brow with the palm of her hand, and soon had the satisfaction of seeing her sink into a deep and quiet sleep.

XIII.

YEARS ago the touch of Teresa, that soothed the troubled mind of Isabel, and toned down the weird reality of hallucination to the playful, kitten-like illusion of a school-girl's dream, would have been accounted magical; now the eager disciple of Mesmer would point to it as another proof of that mysterious power that one person may exercise over another, resolving the world into a blank, and the afflicted person, mind and body, into a figure of wax; or the enthusiastic spiritualist, bridging the mighty chasm between the living and the dead with his dribbled carcass and attenuated soul, would exhibit it as another manifestation of the spiritual agency; but the fact needs no explanation to warrant the truth of this story; if it did, it would be simply on the physiological basis that the force at work to produce the hallucination was perverted from the brain to the brow, expended through the circulation, till, the normal condition of the body restored, a calm, sweet, natural sleep, was the result. Whatever the reason, however, Isabel lapsed from excitement and agitation into quiet sleep, as Teresa drew her hand gently across her brow; and in the depth of an unruffled sea of slumber, passed the night.

The day broke—the little cherub of the dawn went tripping along the scattered clouds in the eastern sky, tipping their ragged edges with gold at his Midas touch, and scattering his rose-petals far and wide with his sportive spendthrift hand. Yet Isabel woke not—though a pale-pink rose-petal fell on her cheek, and rippled its serenity into a smile.

The sun rose; a flood of light rolled over the world, whose actinic wave set myriads of living forms into motion; but Isabel lay unmoved—so still, and the gentle heaving of her breast with every breath so faint and regular, that Teresa gave her an uncertain look before she was satisfied she gazed not on a corpse—the spectral bride of Zomara.

And hour after hour, till four were passed, the sun rose in the heavens, and the old stone dial in the garden registered, before Isabel awoke.

The Seven Sleepers in one, and awakened at last,—said Teresa, with as cheerful a look and tone as she could command, when she saw Isabel's eyes open with the brightness of a three-year old child's.

What, Teresa, returned already, and in merry mood?—replied Isabel, on the instant, but, as if on reflection, and confusion following a contrast of the brighter aspect of the present with the dark and grim gloom of the past, adding—Merry, said I? So the sun shone brighter on my awakening? But a mist rises before my eyes.

No, my lady,—said Teresa, with the same cheerful voice.—The sun shines brighter, the world is glad, and Teresa is among the number of mortals who rejoice.

Rejoice! What a strange sense or feeling!

No, my lady, not strange, since I have seen you sleep so long and so sweetly, and awake looking so refreshed. 'Tis long, indeed, since mirth dwelt with us between these walls, and your voice rang with song and laughter from morn till night; but the

night is passed; another day has dawned; then let us meet and greet its sunshine with reflective spirits, and happiness ever more be our dole.

'Tis true, I feel refreshed, Teresa,—replied Isabel,—but memory still lodges in this poor, distracted globe, and passion frets and throbs with every heart-beat in my bosom—I cannot forget till head and heart are—nay, till my very being is no more! Rejoice? and talk of happiness again? Mockery! mockery! But, Teresa, you know not that in your absence I have seen Zomara?

Nay, this is mockery, my lady; Zomara—

But hear me, Teresa. I have seen Zomara—here, in this chamber, and only yester eve, scarce half an hour before, as I remember now, you returned, and repeated his words.

Alas! my lady, I repeated your own words. If you saw Zomara, and heard him speak, you saw and heard—

A ghost!—concluded Isabel, with a promptness and decision that startled her companion.

A creature of phantasy, my lady; a spectre of a disturbed and disordered imagination—

Define it as you please; but it was Zomara, in form and feature as like him as the Santiago, that leads the Spaniards to victory to-day, is like the Santiago that lived and breathed a thousand years ago. It was Zomara's ghost. There is no doubt now, Teresa. The sea has given up its dead, and Zomara is of them.

'Tis true, my lady, Zomara is dead, and woe! woe! the evil hour he met his terrible fate. But beware his ghost, my lady; it may lead to your destruction.

To destruction? No; you know not, then, that in a moment of despair and desperation, I held Zomara's dagger to my heart, and was about to—

Horrible! horrible! Oh, say no more, dear Isabel!

But Zomara rose before me, and with love, tenderness and pity in his every motion, took the dagger from my hand, pressed it thrice to his lips, and solved the enigma of its several symbols.

Blessed interposition, ghost or goblin!

Amen! Now the dagger no more will intimate death, but life, and love, and faith. It will reconcile me to my lonely fate, sad and sorrowful though it be; for I never can be happy; never, Teresa, till weary, worn out nature releases me from the thraldom of the injunction, and unites us, ghost and ghost, spectre and spectre, soul and soul, or what you will.

Alas! my lady, I marvel at your speech!

It savors of delirium, does it?

Too much like sense. Delirium I understand, but reason—

Smacks of madness. But I have done, Teresa. Mad or otherwise, we will not discuss that now. I do feel refreshed. I have had convictions before, but never felt strong enough to declare them. Why, how brightly the sun does shine this morning. Assist me in my toilet, Teresa. To breakfast, then, a walk.

Teresa gave her a helping hand, but in such a mechanical manner, that showed her thoughts did not accompany her actions. She was still in amaze at the revelation of contemplated suicide by Isabel, at the story of the apparition, and at the decided effect the spectre had on her mind. She feared the melancholy of the suffering woman had been developed into insanity, as her action and reasoning, so unexpectedly to her, seemed to indicate. She pondered over a course to pursue, and determined to acquiesce in her expressions, until she could inform her father, Altanero, and summon the pompous old doctor, Quesada, to ascertain exactly and positively the disease and the danger.

And Teresa was not altogether in the wrong. The condition of Isabel's mind was not healthy, as indicated by her train of thought, expressions, and her suicidal tendencies; and Teresa knew this; to say nothing of what she expected after the long and deep sleep following the excitement and agitation witnessed the evening before. But Isabel's mind was not so much unsettled as Teresa supposed. The profound sleep had been of great benefit to her; and had she been allowed to reflect alone when she awoke, instead of being led into a controversy about that which was most exciting to her, she doubtless would have recovered a tone of mind and body at least one remove from melancholia. It is an easy thing to set up a diseased action again, even after recovery, in many disorders of the brain, much less after only a turn for the better.

You have forgotten one thing,—said Isabel, as Teresa was about to lead the way from the private apartment of Isabel to the breakfast room.

What, my lady?

The token of Zomara. I must wear it next my heart.

Oh, no, my lady; let me guard it now!

Ah, you fear me, Teresa? You have just cause—it is a dagger—and I am mad! So you think, dear, devoted friend. But—Well, well—but guard it as your life, and mine, if you love me.

And, with this last exhibition of hesitation and indetermination, Teresa was confirmed in her opinion that she should reveal what she knew to Don Altanero and Lady Mariana; which she did, save the attempt to take her own life, so terrible an extremity, she could not break her parents' hearts with its recital; but enough she told to alarm them at once, and Martin was forthwith sent for Dr. Quesada, and for Alvaro, now Quesada's warmest friend and most congenial companion, in consultation.

XIV.

MARTIN, on his way to Quesada's, bustled in and out of the alleys of the old town, as nimble as St. Germain's needle, and as anxious as nimble to be seen by as few persons as possible; for his clothing was in a most forlorn condition, and he was ashamed of the sorry figure he cut on the street. He was not too busy, however, to ponder over his condition, situation, affairs, and projects, but meditated about as follows—

First, I am sober. It is a great satisfaction to a man at the outset of an undertaking, to know that he is perfectly sober and master of all his senses and other resources. It is a great satisfaction, but—well, my past life would belie me if I said otherwise—I would as lief dispense with a part of the satisfaction, if not all of it, at present.

Second, I am in rags. Well, that's my master's fault, not mine. I can fall down and sleep where I please, however, without any serious damage to my clothes. Virtue, moreover, is always represented in rags. But the comfort in this, too, I could as well dispense with. I would rather wear velvet and be a passable sinner, than peer through the port holes of poverty, a saint.

Third, I am in love. I will call it love, at any rate, as no other word at my disposal will convey the confusion I feel. I cannot say Nona is beautiful—verjuice and saffron forbid; I cannot say she is young and tender—adjectives will change their significance in years; nor can I say she is lively and gay—confound the rheumatism, say I; but to have her courted by Pedro, and kissed for years, right under my nose—Oh, no, Martin, no quibbling with thyself; how could she be kissed under thy nose by any body but thyself? Well, I have kissed her—there's no gainsaying that; but, 'pon my word, I cannot say there was much delight in it, except to get even with that shadow of a shotten shad, Pedro. But here's the rub—Nona does love that shadow! Why or wherefore, I cannot say. But my belief is simply this—he has given her a philter. And now—

Fourth, I must get an antidote, or a stronger powder, to give her myself.

With this conclusion, Martin reached the house of Dr. Quesada, and in a few minutes more was in the presence of the learned physician.

Can you cure rheumatism?—began Martin, forgetting the prime object of his mission, and a little confused as to his own conclusions.

Cure? No, my good man; not cure. Quacks cure; physicians make no such pretensions.

Then what do you charge for, and pocket the fattest of fees?—inquired Martin, replying, by way of an argument.

For doing what they can to relieve and to restore—for treating patients, not diseases. But, my good man—Martin, I believe, Don Altanero's butler—what would you with me this morning?

Can you cure love?—continued Martin.

Cure love? Well, without fear of being classed with charlatans, I think I could cure love, and without much difficulty. There is within this little vial what, every drop of it, would—

Ah, if it would only cure rheumatism, too!—sighed Martin.

What! lives there a man or woman who loves, and is afflicted with rheumatism?

There is—a woman,—replied Martin.

A curiosity most rare! Why, my good man, I must secure her for the museum, pickle her in wine—

And a pretty pickle you'd make of it. Were the sea wine, and you were to cast her in it, she'd drain it dry! I might assist her a little, of course, but—

Ah, you rogue! But wine and women—the old story—till one is racked with rheumatism, and the other in—

Robes a little the worse for the wear.

Well, my good man, your readiness commands my services, if not your meagre purse. What is your errand?

A remedy for rheumatism and for love,—said Martin, relapsing to the old theme.

Then take it and begone,—and giving the only remarkable significance to this speech with his cane, which he brought down over the shoulders of the astonished butler, the pompous old Æsculapian joker roared out with laughter,—The best remedy for rheumatism and love ever discovered!

Heroic treatment,—added the ready Martin, smarting under the blow, but appreciating the humor of the doctor nevertheless.

To be repeated pro re nata,—continued Quesada, raising his cane and threatening, with assumed anger, to strike again.

Rather, ad nauseam!—said Alvaro, in a deep, stern voice, as he entered and beheld the pompous old doctor and the scallawag butler, burlesquing in such a ludicrous manner the profession, which, in its most profound and serious character, he typified just then himself.

Yes, thanks, my lord,—said Martin;—one dose will do.

No more, Martin. Your mission fulfilled, return to your master. Present Alvaro's compliments, and say he will do himself the honor to wait on him this afternoon.

But, my lord—

No questioning and arguing; go.

But Isabel—my lady—

Well, what of her? I saw her in the garden but an hour ago; she is better than I have seen her for a year.

No, my lord, not well; she—

Has rheumatism, and is in love!—broke in Quesada, laughing the while.

Alas, no, most learned doctor,—said Martin;—she is mad!

Mad!

A lunatic—a maniac—or what you will; but crazy she is beyond doubt. Twice yesterday evening she saw the ghost of Zomara, became wild with excitement, of course; and, as if to put a capping-sheaf to her melancholy, is now mad. 'Tis true, she looks brighter this morning than she has for a year and more, ate her breakfast, and chatted in a woman-like way, without much sense or substance in her discourse, but every now and then her craziness would crop out in a word, a look, or an action, so well marked and unusual, that it was observed by everybody on the instant.

Alas, if this be true!—sighed Alvaro, raising his hand to his forehead, and thereby concealing the cold sweat that was oozing from his brow.

So true, my lord, that I have been sent by my heart-broken master, to inform the doctor and yourself to meet in consultation this morning, and determine on some course of treatment for her forthwith.

Ah, you knave! that my cane had broken your back! What! come you here with such sad news, and jest with me about her rheumatism and love! What scurvy villainy and mockery is this! I'll have you striped till your back looks more like a latticed veranda, or the wires of a parrot's cage, than the case of a Christian!

My lord, and worthy doctor, I crave your forgiveness. But I thought there was no haste.

You'll be a much longer time about curing her, than I in telling you, most profound physician, of the malady, not of my lady Isabel, but of her poor serving-maid, Noma.

The readiest rogue in Spain!—exclaimed Quesada.—Ah, you dog, the lash will be too brief a punishment for you!

Long enough before I am submitted to it, I hope,—rang in Martin.

I'll have you put to the rack!—roared the haughty doctor, becoming exasperated beyond measure.

Thank you, most humane physician; I've been at rack and manger for several years, and not dead yet; to be at rack alone will be a great relief.

Out! out! before—

But Alvaro stepped before the enraged old doctor, withheld his upraised cane, and bade him desist, which he did, as nimble Martin went skipping away at a safe distance, and further demonstrations of such a truculent character only made him appear ridiculous.

Hold, worthy friend,—said Alvaro, gravely.

But the insolence.

Nay; he meant no insolence.

But the sauce—

Seasoned, perhaps, with too much spice and gall; but to your palate's fancy, you must confess, when in the humor of it.

But out of humor—

Well, out of humor, and irritating—exasperating—outrageous, if you will, his conduct and speech were more worthy your contempt than anger.

True, Alvaro; and to you alone would I admit it so freely. Now, let us consider this sad case.

Sad, indeed, it is, if true; but, truly, I do not give it any credence.

Your reasons, Alvaro; for in this matter your profound thought must have resolved itself into those set formula we call reasons.

Yesterday—replied Alvaro—I had an interview with Isabel myself. I pressed my suit with earnestness. We talked of Zomara—we talked freely of him. She was sad, very sad, it is true;

but not so downcast and heart-broken as not to heed me, and give answer to my every question as rationally as ever woman spoke. Nay, she even appointed a day, but two weeks hence, whereon she will decide my fate. Now, doubtless, on my withdrawal, her mind wandered back to Zomara, and in fancy she saw him stabbed in the dark, and cast into the sea by some villain in the service of the king, for such is her theory of the murder, as is the current belief, in fact. Possibly some horrible nightmare possessed her dreams last night, and now haunts her by day. But insane, I cannot believe it for a minute.

Your logic is correct, my philosophic friend; but as a physician, I ignore all logic, except the patient himself or herself. To practice by theory will do in the closet, but not in the sick-chamber. To the individual alone, his or her relationships, condition, age, temperament, and the thousand and one particulars that belong to each individual case, must the physician direct his wisdom and skill. Now, for my part, I will see poor Isabel in person to-day, converse with her on topics that will develop her insane ideas, if she has any; at the same time, feel her pulse, observe the pupil of the eye, mark its glare and expression, as also the cast of the countenance, &c.,—all which can be learned at a glance, as it were, at the bed-side, that a year of Martin's descriptions could not portray as accurately, if ever at all.

You are right, Quesada; we must come to conclusions only from an examination of Isabel herself.

So, in the course of the day, when Isabel could not possibly detect the design to test her supposed insanity, Quesada and Alvaro journeyed over to Don Altanero's, and were soon in the company of, and in conversation with, Isabel. The physician and the philosopher, however, were not long in making up their minds that, far from being insane, she was rather the reverse, a thoroughly sane woman, with a little too much affection, and entirely too much constancy in her composition—a combination here considered a malady that in more modern days might be reckoned an exclusive rarity and a blessing.

XV.

DURING the two weeks intervening between the date of the visit of Quesada and Alvaro to test Isabel's insanity, and the day appointed by her whereon she would give a final answer to Alvaro's suit, it can be readily supposed the latter was in a strange suspense, while the latter lapsed into the indifference of melancholy. Alvaro was in a continual study, deep and distracting in its diverging results. He loved Isabel with the intensity and impetuosity of his nature, and yet he doubted his affection. His admiration for her character was unbounded, yet, upon a close and microscopic analyzation of its details, he lost confidence, became perplexed and troubled. Again, however much she esteemed him as a friend, and admired him as a scholar and philosopher, he was painfully aware of the fact that she did not love him, but the man—horrible, agonizing thought!—whom he had murdered! He felt the wrong he was doing purity and virtue by seeking to unite it with vice and crime. Yet, upon a critical examination of his own character, he was satisfied the good outweighed the evil, and that should decide the character of the whole. He was correct, too, in this opinion of himself; for, however grave his crimes, they were such in his relation to society, and owing as much to chance and circumstance as himself, and not to any innate evil in his heart. The aim of his philosophy was good, the impulse of his being was good; but his will was wavering and his judgment weak; and when excited, if his forces were directed in a proper channel, all was well, but if in an improper groove, all was wrong, till a general crash ensued —wreck and ruin. So, in his aim to win the hand of Isabel, it was not altogether love that urged him on, nor admiration, nor reason,—but back and below all, a sense of man's insignificance in the universe, the creature of the merest chance, unfathomable in intent and ultimate object; it was this that impelled him—fatality! It seemed to him there was but one orbit for the globe of his being to revolve in—or rather, one tangent for the comet of his mass of contrary thoughts and feelings to fly off at, and that was toward Isabel. Love to him was but a circumstance—a force propelling toward her; as was her worth and beauty another circumstance—another force attracting to her. He saw himself the shuttle-cock of fate, accepted, and gave loose rein, accordingly, to thought and passion; nothing was too profound or immense to be considered by his mind; no feeling or passion too engrossing or terrible to be allowed full sway; hence, doubtful, daring, and dangerous, either a god or a devil. And nobody could be more conscious of his character than he was himself. And here came in his substratum of fatality to reconcile him to himself in his philosophy—Are not evil and good so nearly balanced in external nature that the latter is in excess of the former only as life is over death? then why should not the same be so nearly balanced within myself, the same struggle there between good and evil, as there is of life and death? Am I not a microcosm in fact, as far as the less can resemble the greater?

It would be interesting to further analyze this intense mirror of the outer world within his inner self; it would be interesting to take you into his secluded apartment in the old ancestral, castellated mansion, where, amid tomes of lore, works of art, and instruments of research and discovery, in dire disorder, his reflective being gave expression in some thought and emotion; and it would be interesting to lead you with him in his lonely walk through flowery field and woodland wild; along the beach, where wreck and wrack are tangled together, and skulls and shells are tossed alike by the careless waves; or out on the lone sea itself, in a frail bark, with the wave of death beneath and the sky of eternity above; but the dry details of description drag drearily along when action and excitement are anticipated, so, however interesting, at this time it will be forgone.

So, with regard to Isabel, or, also, Teresa. It would be interesting to read page after page of the volume of their hearts, as thoughts and feelings were written down; but the title here only must

be glanced at, and the volume replaced on the shelf—with regret, however, for there is something about this book, this record of silent teachings, like the outlines of fern leaves in shale, or the cobwebs of frost on the midnight pane, that attracts like the weird and mysterious—the love of woman, pure, holy, wronged and suffering woman, possesses a charm that awes all ages and climes.

Nay, let us not replace this volume in the case in haste; there is time enough to at least glance at these pictures on opposite pages as the book opens before us. Ah, this is Melancholy pacing through the garden with uncertain and unheeded step, treading under foot the dainty daisies of delight, the sweet pansies of thought, even the budding roses of hope, and, alas! now a bleeding heart! And this is Despair, wildly wandering in the dark, tearing up by the roots the daffodills of designs defeated, the holly of hope blasted and sear, and sowing instead briar and thorn. 'Tis strange, too, the faces of the twain so unlike, seem to dissolve, blend together, and, at length, exchange identities—Isabel and Teresa at one time; Teresa and Isabel at another. So, could you but read the accompanying text, the woman hearts of both these loving women, so distinct and diametrically opposite in their directions, would thence appear confounded and confused, and not perhaps only one with the other, but also with your own. Ah, that touches to the quick? Well, now put the book up, ponder and dream; perhaps, by some metempsychosis, thou art, or Isabel, or Teresa, or both.

And now let us step forward to the end of the two weeks indicated above, which concludes a period of one and twenty months, or thereabout, since the exciting day and thrilling night that witnessed the first scenes of the story.

XVI.

ON the day appointed by Isabel to express her final favor, or disfavor, of Alvaro's suit, Don Borracho, the high-living, generous and impulsive father of Alvaro, made his appearance at his friend Altanero's at an early hour. He was accompanied as usual by a rich gift of wines and viands, and an elegant and extravagantly expensive present for Isabel. Pedro, as usual, too, carried these gifts, and, with the assistance of Nona, as might be presumed, displayed them on the side-board with similar manipulations, manoeuvres, and adventures, as were detailed at the setting of this truthful history.

The nearly two years that had elapsed, had made little change on either of these two persons. Pedro was as distortedly philosophic as ever, and as droll and deliberate; while his capacity for wine was only measured by his ability to get at it. The real character of this old mortal, this born bur-lesque of wisdom and philosophy, and living sem-blance of dead and denyed thought and feeling, resembled more a grim and grotesque Indian idol, enclosed within a well-worn and corroded shell, which I have seen, than anything I can think of. He provoked not laughter altogether, but rather a humorous amazement. Nona, on the other hand, was neither grotesquely philosophic nor amazingly humorous, but quite different. With fifty years experience within the walls of the household, she had not learned much, nor a variety; but what she did acquire, held on to it well—even the rheu-matism, making its acquaintance at least twenty years ago, she kept it green in her memory, as she did an imagined blight to her affection of fully fifteen years longer standing. She took things as they came, accordingly, with an indifference and passiveness highly gratifying to Pedro and Martin, who, in turn, during the other's absence, could en-joy exclusively the delights of her conversation, the embrace of her rheumatic arms, and press their lips with ecstatic bliss against her cheek—her cheek, in color, consistency, and comfort, like a cold buckwheat cake.

Well, after Borracho had arrived, and Altanero and he had sampled a bottle or two of his richest wine, as was their wont, they sat down at a table to while away the hours in a social game. But the game of itself gave little interest to Altanero, and soon he suggested a stake, which was accepted by the generous Don, of course; and loud and long

rang the laughter of the jovial old fellow as he won again and again in tolerably rapid succession. But as Borracho won, Altanero plied him with his own wine, and connived at Pedro's marginal notes—so to speak—which he detected him in tak-ing down, till at length both master and man were tight and unconscious of the ruse and deceit he was practising.

Pedro, help your master and yourself to wine,—said Altanero.—Let its warm, rich life infuse itself into these well-worn frames and sluggish veins, until our boyish days come back to us—the days when we knew not the meaning of passion, of poverty and pride, when, with keen appetites, we passed from pleasure to pleasure, too careless to analyze, too busy to regret. Fill up, old comrade, ere we play again, and let us drink to the old, old days.

Yes, wine! Pedro!—cried out Borracho, raising his hand above his head to bring it down by way of emphasis on the table, showing plainly, mean-while, his cards to the keen-eyed Altanero.—Yes, wine! Give me wine, for wine loves me, and I love it! To forget is happiness. He is a fool who would not drink, for by the cup we become rich, well clothed, well fed, aye, kings of wealth and power unreached by common sovereigns. Wine, Pedro, give me wine!

But not new wine into old bottles, else they break—their necks,—said Pedro, with increasing familiarity, as the wine began to warm him up and thaw out the iceberg of his wit and humor, to float down the current of the conversation of the occasion, till, melted away entirely, it disap-peared in the surrounding kindred flood. But Pedro, nevertheless, filled the glasses, and took another swig himself aside, as he uttered his phil-osophic signal of warning.

Yes, philosophy, even from Pedro, is philoso-phy—said Borracho, with affected solemnity and gravity,—You are young, Pedro, and remember this, you must hold the wine—not the wine hold you. Drinking will not hurt a man; only fools, who know not how to drink, suffer.

But Borracho, by this time, had taken a little too much, and an ominous swaying of the body, as well as a stammer and hesitation in his speech, gave an intimation to Altanero that his scheme had been frustrated by overdoing the plying of wine. The cursed old fool is drunk,—muttered Altanero to himself—His philosophy is a sure sign of his loss of reason.

Now, comrade,—began Altanero, in a loud voice, as if to wake the drowsy Borracho to another instant of comprehension before he fell into insensibility,—now for the play which makes one of us the winner! There is the king of spades—

But it was too late. Borracho did open one eye about full, and the other possibly a little more than half way, but a drunken drowsiness had overcome him; his eyelids closed with a sidelong and uneven wink, exasperating in the extreme, with a droll expression of, You can't come it! in it; and, in another minute, he fell forward on the table like a heavy inanimate thing, dead drunk, as the saying is.

Curse on the luck!—soliloquized the thwarted Altanero, in the secrecy of his self-seclusion,—Curse the luck! I have been losing to lead him on, and now he falls senseless when I begin to win. The last of my high-bred horses goes to his well-filled stables to pay for this morning's entertainment.

Rising from the table, highly chagrined and exasperated, and turning toward Pedro, leaning against the sideboard, almost as drunk as his master, he began to vent his spleen on him.

Harkee, sirrah!—said he, with satire curling his thin upper lip, and bitterness bearing down the nether,—You feel proud of your rich master, do you not?—he continued, with contempt contracting the ridge of his nose, and distending his nostrils like lateral flaps.— Yours should be a well paid service,—he added, his haughtiness hoisting up the right eyebrow and depressing the left, leaving the ball of his right eye free and distinct from the lid like a staring full moon of wonder, and the left half concealed, like a sullen scowl and lurking threat.

But the grotesque mound-idol of philosophy heeded not this visage of wrath and gall, but stammered out—Time is money, my lord. Money is power. My time is his money and his power. The laborer is worthy of his hire.

True, you knave, and I have wasted precious time both with master and with man,—said Altanero.—Now, remove your master to a chamber, that he may find in slumber a partial renewal of his powers. Out with him!

But Pedro was too much intoxicated to move from his support, so that he stood staring intensely grave and solemn at the frowning Altanero, and looking, the while, like an antiquated and distempered parrot with a salaam palsy.

Altanero then summoned Martin and other assistants, and had the twain removed—a delightful occupation to Martin, that part of it which pertained to removing Pedro, for he could take the advantage to punch him under the ribs to his heart's content, jam his head against the side of the doorway in taking him through it, rifling his pockets of any money that might be there, and, above all, get a chance at the wines on the sideboard himself.

May he awake to forgetfulness of his winnings,—said Altanero to himself, as Borracho was carried from the room, —small to him, but great to one as poor as Altanero! What a maddening curse is poverty itself, but when wedded with pride, harrowing in the extreme! But,—thought he, as he paced to and fro across the room, and the occasion of Borracho's coming that morning recurring to his mind,—I could retrieve my fortunes, if once this marriage of Alvaro with my daughter could be consummated. And, by the way, this is the very day, appointed by herself, after nearly two years of woman-whinings over the death of Zomara, on which she was to give Alvaro a final answer to his suit. I will send for her. She shall marry him. Why, there's not such another match for her in Spain—years, culture, honor, and fortune, and, at least, communion of friendship and esteem, from which love will grow when they learn each other's worth, as certainly as the bud develops into the full-blown rose. But no matter; she shall marry him! Nor do I injustice to my love for her, in this. For oh, what agony the thought to leave, at my death, my only and beloved child, a tender and most noble daughter, unprovided for, when circumstance and opportunity thrust this princely competency before her for acceptance. Yes, she shall marry him. I have sworn it, by the proud name I bear, and no obstacle shall stand to break that oath!

Altanero then called Martin, and bade him bear to Isabel his love, and wish that she attend him in the parlor. Martin looked despairingly at the wine as he passed it on the sideboard, but his master's eye was on him, and he passed on.

We shall see now,—thought Altanero, as he seated himself, and began to tighten the screws of his dictation and sternness,—we shall see, now, in what mind we find the stubborn lady. Her obstinacy would make a saint forget affection.

Most loved and respected sir, at your command, I wait,—began Isabel, as she reached almost the chair of her father before he was aware of her presence, so silent was her entrance and motion across the room.

And is there no softer word,—asked Altanero, harshly,—in your vocabulary, my most loving and respectful daughter, that you must choose the harsh and grating word, "command," in indicating your unwilling acquiescence in my humble wish to see you?

Dear father,—said poor Isabel, trembling; such unkindness and injustice to her from her father being so unusual,—sorrow and perplexity have so racked your daughter's mind as to leave her weak to choose where her foot may fall when walking, much less to mark the words which hardly flutter through her lips to the unresponsive air.

Come, my child,—said Altanero, softening, giving way entirely to his affection for his daughter, and beginning to tremble himself, as he became conscious of the unwarranted harshness he had been guilty of,—come, my child, a truce alike to melancholy thoughts and to unseemly encounters upon words, which are, at best, but poor and uncertain messengers of our thoughts.

Then kissing her fondly, as if to give her an assurance of his affection that could not be doubted, he bade her sit down and feel composed and comfortable, while he disclosed his object in sending for her at that time.

Isabel,—he calmly said,—I wished to see you this day, appointed by yourself, to learn the welcome news that Alvaro's suit had met with your acceptance. I have told you how the revenues, by which our family once matched sovereigns in pomp and hospitality, have wasted slowly and inevitably, under the proud and generous hands of successive generations. If Alvaro receives your hand, we can walk again with confidence and pride these halls, whose atmosphere is laden with grand traditions of our once regal splendor; and your poor old father, the last of his race, can go to his final rest, peacefully, because your future is assured; thankfully, because Providence, in making him poor, yet gave him a daughter; proudly, because the sacred and honorable inheritance received by him may be, by him, delivered up to a worthy successor, undiminished and unstained. If you refuse his suit, my mind, long used to other thoughts, knows not how to draw that death, in hovel, poverty and wretchedness, which awaits a poor and broken-hearted husband and father, who leaves without shelter or care, to the cold charities of an unfeeling world, the wife of his bosom and the tender child—the sole remaining fruit of a life-long love. I await confidently your reply, for you are a true daughter of the Altaneros, and desire our proud continuance.

Father, spare me now,—said Isabel, faintly, overcome at the terrible alternative of her father's remarks, which she must meet and decide upon that day,—spare me now, dear father. I am not strong. But I will try to do my duty.

I will, my daughter,—replied Altanero.—You need not answer me, but when Alvaro comes, you must have strength enough to make us all happy.

Altanero then withdrew from the room, as Lady Mariana and Teresa entered, and approached Isabel.

Yes; I may as well here remark the haggard look of wretchedness in the countenance and carriage of Teresa, for her fate hung, as well as others, on the decision of Isabel, as you may well imagine, knowing the secret history of her heart as you do.

My poor girl,—asked Lady Mariana,—have you, as I bade you, sought counsel and guidance of Heaven? The blessed promise, ask and it shall be given you, is not an empty one, nor does the good book mock us when it says, as thy days, so shall thy strength be.

Yes, mother, I have prayed,—answered Isabel, —oh, how often and earnestly!—that I might be enabled to see my duty, as pointed out by father, by you, and by our necessities; but all is still deep darkness, without one ray of light.

God thus seeks,—said Lady Mariana,—to uproot sweet yet sinful attachments, which divide with Him the dominion of our hearts. Isabel, I once suffered, as you now do, but, praise be to our Lady of Grace and her Blessed Son, I found at last that peace which passeth all understanding. I believe that you will find this rest, for I have prayed, night after night, for your deliverance from doubt.

All is so dark,—sighed Isabel,—so dark, and, as I grope along, the outstretched hand finds no guide, the faltering feet no firm earth to stand upon. If it were not a sin, I would rather pray our Father to take back the sorrowing soul which scarcely animates my weakened body.

Peace, my child,—concluded Lady Mariana,— wrong not Him, who doeth all things well. I will leave you with Teresa, whose firmer nature and more experienced mind, will strengthen you for the duty which yet remains to be done.

Lady Mariana then left the room, and Isabel fell on Teresa's neck.

O Teresa! Teresa! what shall I do? My father, my mother, constrain me, their necessities are urgent, and Alvaro, who asks my hand, and who loves me as his life, is all that a woman could wish her lover to be. Yet I feel that, should I consent, I would wrong my own soul and the dear memory of the dead. What can I do, Teresa?

Alvaro—all a woman could wish her lover to be!—sighed Teresa in secret.—Come not to me,

my lady, for how can I, to whom the world's almost unknown, explain the hidden mysteries of the heart? Why one should desire, another detest; one sue for, another reject? None but God, by whom our natures are given, can solve the eternal problem of love.

Alvaro will be here ere long. There is no escape for me, and yet I know not what to do.

This I have read, my lady,—replied Teresa,— that Love will clothe its object, without reason, with all that's worthy of itself; and that there is no greater grief than for Love to be rudely awakened from its dream with the knowledge that it has bestowed itself on one unworthy—awakened, too, when it has spent its wealth and power upon the stony heart of selfishness.

Martin here announced the arrival of Alvaro, kept his eye on the wine, and while Isabel and Teresa were still conversing, managed to slip a bottle from the board and under his coat, and look as unconcerned about it as if he had done some minor act of duty.

He is here,—sighed Isabel.—Heaven help me! Now, Teresa, leave me awhile.

And leave all hope behind,—thought Teresa, as she withdrew to the back of the room where, supposing her presence would pass unheeded, unseen and unheard, she waited, with breathless suspense, the interview.

Bid him enter, Martin,—said Isabel, mustering to her aid whatever calmness she could control.

Martin retired, and presently Alvaro entered, with a kind and confident tone in his bearing and speech, that inspired a little more confidence in Isabel herself.

Ah,—sighed Teresa, as she saw the proud form of the man she loved with such intensity that endured all woe with its continuance, now about to offer himself a husband to the woman whom, next to herself, he had wronged most grievously. —What finer clay—she asked herself—and loftier spirit unite to form the nobleman and privilege him to blast the love and life of the peasant girl, and, with imperious will, to choose his bride among the fairest and the noblest of the land?

Alvaro advanced confidently to Isabel, bowed, took her hand courteously in his own, and pressed it tenderly to his lips.

I salute you, fair lady. By your own appointment, and spurred by continual devotion, I am here to lay again at your feet my wealth, my title, and my life, and to learn whether they are worthy of the kind regard of her whose smile will repay for all.

Alvaro, you still press me for an answer?—said Isabel, half inquiringly and half reprovingly.

Yes, Isabel; for, secluded as you have been from all society save that of older persons or menials, I can understand why, when you are asked to decide a matter affecting your weal or woe for life, you are in doubt and hesitate to speak the final word. But think of, Isabel, the two years' torment I have suffered; think, that more than twenty times the moon has waxed and waned, and twice the earth performed its circuit round the sun, since I placed, with your father's favor, my suit before you; think, that my love has been uncomplaining; that its patience has equaled its depth; that I have not vexed you with importunate lover's arts; that I have, without murmur, waited until this day, your own choice, to hear the words which determine my future.

Alvaro, I have indeed reason to thank you for your forbearance. I always have regarded you as a friend,—one, who to me would be kind and careful beyond all around me. When we were children, we have climbed the mountains, and crossed, on uncertain stones, the brawling streams. Always you guided, supported, and protected me. Later, when in my studies, inexperience had failed to solve perplexities, I found you ever a sure resort. And now, will you bear with me, and hear a doubt which disturbs me?

If anything that my poor powers may discern,—replied Alvaro,—will aid you, joy and pride will accompany their exercise.

You know, then, that Zomara had my love; that to him my first and best love clung; that at his death the pulse of affection within me ceased. Can you hope for happiness from union with the ashes of affection, with the skeleton of love? Why do you wish this wreck to be your wife?

On what has the love-laden vessel been shattered,—argued Alvaro.—You knew this hero for a few weeks when you were but a child, and lavished upon him the wealth of your affection. He is dead. Now you, with youth, beauty, and position, would bury yourself in the grave of an unknown—aye, would drag with you your aged father and saintly mother. Isabel, let the result of my careful study of the human heart tell you that true love is begotten by long and constant intercourse, by years of intimacy, by community of tastes and studies, by mutual experience and united interests, by that charm which is the growth of the companionship of proven worth and unquestioned beauty; all these conditions have been ours and dictate our union. Further, your father's comfort and your mother's happiness, both dear to you, impel you to be mine. I promise you that they shall be my constant care, when I have acquired the right to minister unto them; that they shall know no wish ungratified—no sorrow that precaution can prevent; they shall, in their old age, enjoy that peace which is the true transition from this life to eternity; and, when they see their only child loved, and earnestly cared for, by one whose wealth, and power, and life, are all subservient to her, they will pass away from earth with calm and sweet satisfaction. Think of all this, dear Isabel, and believe that where so many good motives direct you to one course, that course must lead you to peace and happiness.

Isabel remained in a deep reverie a minute or more before she replied, her pallor increasing, and her weakness becoming more and more evident.

Leave me now,—at length she said, faintly,—and I promise you, Alvaro, that to-morrow shall bring you my answer.

To-morrow?

Yes, to-morrow. My weakness must excuse me now.

To-morrow, then,—said Alvaro, cheerfully, rising, and pressing her fair, cold hand to his lips again,—to-morrow let it be; and bear in mind, meanwhile, dear Isabel, how I yearn to have the right to banish that pallor from your cheek, that weakness from your limbs, and to restore the bloom, the strength and joy which should attend your youth and beauty. Adieu!

Saying which he left the room, and Teresa came forward to Isabel.

O Teresa,—cried out Isabel, as Teresa laid her hand on her shoulder, and twined her raven tresses mechanically around her finger,—why should I uphold longer my weak woman's will against the manifest decrees of Heaven? Since Zomara's death, all hope, all wish, all aim, have left this body, and why should I not give the lifeless form to any one, if, by such an act, I can purchase peace and comfort for the remaining years of my beloved parents?

Poor child! to mourn to one more mournful than yourself,—sighed Teresa, sinking in abject woe, as she saw, at last, that Isabel was about to yield and stand between her and Alvaro—an affianced bride! Till that moment she was confident that Isabel would cling to the memory of Zomara until death, but she perceived now the contrary—breaking down by the force of circumstances, and yielding, however unwillingly, to another—but to one, the assassin of Zomara! and oh, how agonizing the thought! the assassin to whom her being clung with the strong hooks of a love that imbued her whole being and endured all anguish and woe!

With a last, lingering but faint hope, Teresa drew the dagger of Zomara from the belt of Isabel, pressed the hilt against her pallid lips, and fervently said to her—Love Zomara! Trust in God that your love will be requited at last! Yes, love in faith and hope until death!

Love Zomara!—exclaimed Isabel, starting up, seizing the dagger and kissing it with rapturous ecstacy again and again.—Yes, Teresa, I will love Zomara, and Zomara alone, through life and all eternity!

But why stands she motionless, and with fixed gaze directs her staring eyes, as it were, against the blank of space? The apparition of Zomara rises again before her disordered mind! But what bears he upon his shoulders? It is a corpse! It is the corpse of her father! Worn out by her obstinacy, exhausted with care and anxiety for her welfare, he has gone to an untimely grave on the shoulders of a spectral lover!

With this horrible phantasy in her mind, as the spectre of Zomara hurled the corpse of her father into a wretched grave, she uttered a heart-rending shriek and fell insensible to the floor.

XVII.

THE morrow came, and with it courage and determination. It was her duty to sacrifice herself for the welfare of her parents, and Isabel obeyed.

But what means that unwonted brilliancy in the eye of Teresa? What means the repetition by her of Isabel's words—Alvaro is all that a woman could wish her lover to be? What means that suspicion in her gait, and that hesitation in her speech? Can you mistake it? See the glow of her blood through her dark olive skin. It is jealousy enkindled in her bosom!

As long as Isabel was true to Zomara, Teresa had no rival. Alvaro might sue for the hand of Isabel, might worship her; but that, however galling, was endurable when Isabel's heart was adamant against his approaches; but the very instant Isabel yielded, and though she loved her as a pure and holy being, Teresa, forthwith, was fired with jealousy, and a jealousy that burned with such intensity and insatiate greed, that all other thoughts, emotions and passions sank into insignificance beside it.

But toward the end of the day on which Isabel consented to her marriage with Alvaro, and all was excitement and joy in the houses of Altanero and Borracho in consequence, Teresa, brooding alone over her peculiar situation, came to a conclusion and determination that produced a train and sequence of events which will form the great climacteries of this story. But not to anticipate. Nay, be not so impatient. All will transpire in due time.

XVIII.

LET us now go back to Zomara, and see what became of him; for, when toppled over the cliff and into the stormy sea, by Alvaro, he was dropped from this narrative, except so far as his supposed death affected the several interested characters, principally Isabel, Teresa, and Alvaro.

His story is a short one.

You will recollect that Pedro brought up a wrecked pirate, who, after telling who he was, and how he came there, did the very best thing he could do under the circumstances, died, and relieved the government of the trouble and expense of hanging him. Now that should give you a cue. Zomara fell into the sea at the time the waves were beating against the shore, and bearing up the wreck of a pirate vessel, till casks and bales, and lumber, spars and tackle, clothing, weapons, utensils, and such like, were strewn along the beach in such confusion as can result only from a total wreck. And here and there lay the lifeless form of a pirate, or tossed about on the waves against some rugged rocks, bobbing up and down with all the horror that death in this most terrible form can inspire; with now and then, but rarely, a poor fellow lying insensible on a rock where a larger wave has borne him, and no succeeding smaller has been able to bear him away, or clinging, with almost exhausted strength, to some rock on which he is cast, but without strength sufficient to draw himself up to a place of safety. Zomara fell amid this general wreck, just where the wave and shore held alternate sway beneath the more jutting part of the cliff. And there he lay insensible till next morning, when he was picked up, with several of the pirates not yet dead, and carried with them to a prison, to await either death from exhaustion, or, after a trial for piracy, death on the scaffold or gallows.

When Zomara awoke from insensibility, he found himself confined in the cell of a prison in company with a stranger, whom he recognized as a sailor from his dress, and soon found from his speech that he was a wrecked pirate; and, in a short time afterwards, he learned the particulars of the wreck. He was not long, moreover, in ascertaining that the pirate was a maniac, having lost his reason, most probably, on account of the excitement and exhaustion incident to the foundering of the vessel and her breaking up on the coast. But every now and then the poor fellow would shriek aloud, as if feeling the most intense fear and anguish, and, in his ravings, however incoherent, referred continually to some frightful form Zomara knew bore no connection to the wreck. This continued for sometime, when Zomara, curious, and anxious to relieve the terrible suspense he was in, not knowing the cause of his incarceration, but surmising it to be his identification as Zomara, the banished man, inquired directly of the pirate, during a lucid interval, what horrible object it was that haunted his mind?

What!—exclaimed the maniac, starting back, and fixing his staring, glazed eyes intently on the questioner,—do you not see that monster rise from the sea, and stretch an arm like a mizzen mast against the sky! and now another! and another! till—O God, it has lashed an arm about two sailors, and sweeps them from the deck! Aloft! aloft! for your life! But alas! in vain! for the arm sweeps through the rigging and fastens its cold, snake-like being around my body! Help! help! O Holy Mother, help! Aye; it was the gallant captain hurled the first harpoon into the monster! then the mate! and then the men, till seven barbs were quivering deep in its flesh! O God! I faint! My hold loosens! I fall to the deck! But what is this encircles my body, and lies a shapeless mass by my side? It is the arm that tore me from the rigging now severed from the monster's body by the daring crew! Now, hold to the lines! cries out our brave captain! But snap! snap! go the ropes, like whip-cord! and the vessel quivers from stern to stern as they break! The monster disappears to rise no more! The vessel is saved! The cry was heard above even from a pirate in distress! Saved! saved!

A devil-fish!—said Zomara.

A monster devil-fish!—replied the pirate.—Why, sir; we were off the coast of St. Helena. The sky was clear and the sea calm. The captain had ordered the boat to be scrubbed and thoroughly cleaned. A plank was suspended on the side of the vessel, and two of my comrades stood on this plank while scraping and calking the ship. When suddenly the frightful arm rose! The sailors scale the side of the vessel and fly for their lives, but the arm descends and sweeps them into the sea! What! another! and another! Aloft! for your life!

And so on the maniac continued, with semi-sane intervals of longer or shorter durations, in which

But during a paroxysm of his mania, at length, when he reached the acme of his excitement, following a wild shriek that made the prison ring, the pirate suddenly sprang forward and fell dead!

Zomara was now alone in the silence and gloom of a prison. All was as still as death, and as impressive as the terrible death, under the circumstances described, could make it. He listened breathless for the faintest sound, but in vain. Following the noise and tumult of the madman, the silence impressed itself more on his mind than his situation.

But a sense of his whereabouts came at last. He was in Spain! His life was forfeited by disobe-

he would begin his story calmly; but in a short time, as he approached the narration of his own narrow escape, he would lapse into delirium or downright mania.

The exact phrases he uttered I will not attempt to reproduce. Suffice it, they were hurried, incoherent, and extravagant; and all that I care to have you know is, that Zomara, hearing the story repeatedly, and with such variations, till all the circumstances of the extraordinary occurrence were firmly impressed on his memory, could repeat them with the same minuteness of detail, if necessary. And what use he made of his memory will appear in due time.

dience of the king's decree! And he was now helpless in prison, where his life could be taken at any moment, his carcass thrown to the dogs, and nobody, save the king and his hireling, know anything about it! Then came a thought of Isabel, and a recurrence of all that had happened since he landed the day before; and the cry of Isabel again rang in his ears as she saw him stagger backward past her, and fall over the cliff. Alas! he sighed; what grief must be hers! Ah, pure, loving, trusting heart, break not till I can tell you I still live—live!—love!—and hope!

But to make a long story short, Zomara concluded that he had been picked up with the wreck of the pirate vessel, and was supposed to be a pirate himself, and borne, accordingly, with others, with the one lying dead at his feet at any rate, to prison; and presently he concluded that if he could only continue under the mask of a pirate, he might escape death; and possibly the piratical character of the wrecked vessel could not be proven, and he could not only escape with his life, but go free, depart from Spain, and survive, in foreign lands, the term of his banishment; in the meantime communicate with Isabel, if wealth could influence the bearing of a message to her. And it was but one remove, logically, from this thought, to induce him to exchange clothing with the dead pirate, whose identification was of minor moment. So, in a few minutes more, Zomara, to any casual glance, his face concealed, lay dead on the floor, while a crazy pirate, in the darkest corner of the cell, could rave and rant, as he saw fit, best to disguise himself, and carry out any ideas of escape he might have in the future.

Zomara, too, was careful to keep all the money he could find in the pockets of both, knowing full well that it was a key that unlocked, at will, most prisons; and the ring of Isabel he took especial pains to secrete within a fold of his new garment acquired by the exchange.

It was well enough, too, that Zomara completed the exchange and secreting of his money and treasure when he did, for presently he heard the bolt of an outer lock turn, then footsteps approach across the paved hall to the door of his cell, and then the lock of his own door open, when, peering cautiously around, he saw before him the jailer and Alvaro! It was well enough, moreover, that Alvaro had rapidly come from the broad glare of day into the gloom of the cell; for, before his eyes were sufficiently accustomed to the light to see distinctly, he determined that the dead body that lay on the floor, dressed in Zomara's clothes, was Zomara; and forthwith he left the cell. There was a sigh, however, that escaped from his bosom, and a falter in his step, as he turned and withdrew, that told the story of the inner man—murder—horror—remorse—and Alvaro the murderer!

But, my lord,—said the jailer,—what will I do with this carcass?

Bury it immediately, as it is.

Ha! ha! no, my lord; it's a gallus coat this rogue wears—I'll not bury that!

What's the coat worth in money?

A doubloon, at least.

And whatever other clothing of the corpse?

Two more, at the most skinflint pawnbroker's in the kingdom.

Well, here are six doubloons, good jailer. Take them, and bury the clothes of this body with it.

Ha! ha! a gallus gift, my lord; I will, I will.

But you will not deceive me?

Ha! ha! my lord; how long would it take you, for less gold than this, to cut my head from my shoulders? There's many a gallus knave in your own household would cut my weasand for one. But, my lord, you don't fear me?

Fear you? and for what?

Ha! ha! my lord, for not burying or burning the clothing of this—

Pirate.

Pirate! Ha! a gallus pirate! Dressed like a soldier! Ha! ha! a gallus pirate!

No matter; dispose of him as I direct; disobey at your peril.

Saying which, in a stern voice that admitted of no further quibbling, Alvaro left the prison; and the jailer, turning the key on him, uttered his demoniacal laugh again, muttering—some villainy, I'll warrant; or the world has grown very good since I turned jailer. Ha! ha! is the jailer-king a fool? to bury goods that may be gold? Ha! ha! no, my lord, Alvaro—haughty, high and mighty Alvaro! I've got your gold, and I'll have this soldier's clothes too! Ha! ha! a gallus cove is the jailer-king!

Barnabas—for that was the jailer's name—then stripped Zomara's clothes from the dead pirate, and searched them carefully for gold and secreted jewels. Finding nothing, his first suspicion was that the crazy pirate in the corner had not been too crazy to anticipate him in this, and he forthwith accosted him, and made bold to search his

49

person. But Zomara, in the role of the maniac, rose to his full height, and exerting himself to his full strength, seized the burly jailer suddenly, and threw him against the wall of the cell with such force that a vacancy in the jailership seemed imminent for a few minutes after. But only for a few minutes; for Zomara, not following up his advantage gained, and possessing the key of the prison and liberating himself, burst out into an assumed maniacal rant about the devil-fish, and Barnabas was given time to recover from the shock and regain his feet, when he was a match for the strongest man in the kingdom, were he not a coward at heart.

Ha! ha! my crazy cove, I'll bring the madness out of you! Ill tame your strength, my gallus pirate! I'll starve you in this cell till you're as mild and weak as yarn, and you'll sell your soul for a crust of bread! I'll have your gold within a fortnight!

But Zomara pretended to heed not the threat, and continued his raving.

Ha! ha! as crazy a cove as ever I saw! And as strong as a bull! But I'll tame him!

So concluding, Barnabas removed the clothing he had stripped from the pirate, and went away, leaving the carcass in the cell with Zomara the livelong day and the following night. The stench that arose was horrible and sickening; but the high carnival the rats held over the body, leaping with wild delight from one extremity to the other, and nibbling in turn the fingers and toes, the nose, the lips, and the eyelids, was revolting in the extreme. Zomara drove away the ravenous animals again and again; but they went no farther than the crevices between the huge stones of the prison walls, from which they peered with a roguish, devilish delight in their jet black eyes, and renewed their attacks on the carcass at every turn of Zomara's back, or intermission in his vigilance. And this continued till Zomara fell asleep from exhaustion, and the rats had undisputed possession of the body, to bicker and quarrel about it among themselves, till, about dawn, glutted to satiety, they waddled off heavily to their holes, and disappeared.

XIX.

WHEN Barnabas came, in the morning, to remove the carcass of the pirate, he brought with him some bread and water for Zomara's breakfast. But, despite his hunger, having eaten not a morsel for nearly two days, the food was so loathsome and the circumstances so oppressive, Zomara was not able to take a bite. Seeing which, the jailer uttered his demoniacal, derisive laugh, and dragged away the body with as little concern as if it had been a log, took with him the untouched and untasted food, and left Zomara once more to ponder alone over his situation.

In an hour or two after, however, Barnabas returned, and in his company came a judge.

Crazy, say you?—said the judge, in the hall of the prison, but loud enough for Zomara to hear with his intent ear every word.

Ha! ha! hear him rave, and talk about devils! If he be not crazy, I'll sell my head for a bobbin.

But he may be malingering. He knows his doom as a pirate, and to escape it, is perhaps playing the part of a madman.

Ha! ha! go in to the gallus cove alone, and reason with him! Not mad? Ha! ha! he'd devour you in a minute! Did I not show you his food untouched? Ha! ha! and did I not show you how he gnawed at the flesh of his dead comrade in the night? You won't go in?

Not I, good Barnabas.

Then look at him, and see for yourself.

Barnabas threw open the door of the cell, and the judge stepped to the door; but the loathsome stench, that came out in the latter's face, staggered him, and he stepped back into the hall.

Zomara, horrified at the brutality of the jailer, and dreading longer confinement under his savage charge, as a fate more terrible than a thousand deaths, stepped quickly and boldly to the door, and said—

Do not fear me, my lord; I am not mad; I am not a pirate; I am—

But Barnabas, pretending great terror at this juncture, struck Zomara in the face with his heavy key, and sent him back into the cell, laughing out—Ha! ha! I'll teach you to break my back against the walls of your cell! Not a pirate? Ha! a gallus cove to lie.

The terror-stricken judge, too, fled in dismay. The wretched, haggard face of Zomara, as he stooped at the door of his cell to address him, was so forbidding that it was terrible to him, and he hurried away, ready to believe him anything that Barnabas would suggest. The fact, moreover, that he did not find Zomara raving as he expected, was convincing to him of his insanity, for he knew well that malingerers were more apt to burst out into active delirium at the approach of any one than to be quiet and calm.

Zomara was accordingly kept in prison as a crazy pirate—his sentence commuted to imprisonment for life by the humane judge, who ordered the other pirates—for he believed Zomara one of them—to be executed. The pirates, moreover, acknowledged the prisoner who was insane, and raved about an adventure with a devil-fish, as one of them, and satisfied the judge of the humanity of his sentence.

To Zomara, however, the sentence was indescribably terrible. At the mercy of Barnabas! Horrible! horrible!

He saw through the villainy of Barnabas to retain him at least till he had robbed him of everything valuable about his person; for the jewels secreted about the persons of the pirates executed, gave the avaricious jailer ample reason to believe that Zomara, however crazy, did possess, to some degree, that passion which was overruling in him. At the first opportunity, accordingly, Zomara secreted most of the gold he became possessed of when he donned the pirate's clothes, and added thereto what he had himself about him, when he made the exchange. Dividing it into several sums, he concealed the greater part of it in the crevices in the walls and floor of his cell, leaving the remainder in his purse to relieve the jailer of any suspicion. The only hope he had in his despair was that, through the avariciousness of Barnabas,

he might communicate with Isabel by letter or verbal message, agree upon some plan of action, and eventually make good his escape from the prison and from Spain; at any rate, if not to effect his escape, at least to inform her of his situation, and, almost in her presence, wear out the term of his banishment, infinitely preferable than to wander far from her in foreign lands.

In a few days, when he was thoroughly convinced that avarice was the ruling passion in Barnabas, and when he had been reduced, by slow starvation, to a being almost pitifully weak, he whispered gold! in the hearing of the jailer, and immediately a deferential and submissive air was assumed.

Will you bear a message for me?—asked Zomara.

Ha! ha! that I will—for gold! But with whom would you communicate?

Do you know Don Altanero?

What! my lord Altanero, whose mansion stands on the cliff within sight of this prison?

He has a daughter.

My lady, Donna Isabel, the fairest lady in Grenada.

To her would I have you bear a message. Provide me with ink and paper, and this gold piece be your reward.

Ha! ha! a gallus cove! Ha! ha! a gallus pirate! In love with Don Altanero's daughter! Ha! a gallus crazy cove!

No matter; here's the gold piece for your trouble—will you do it?

Ha! ha! that I will—but double it first.

Well, here are two.

Ha! ha! I'll get you paper and ink forthwith;—and, snatching the money, Barnabas retired.

It would be curious to go through the reasoning of Barnabas when he withdrew. He was puzzled about Zomara's insanity that exhibited such lucid intervals; but he was more perplexed to know how a wrecked pirate could know Donna Isabel, much less be in love with her; for he could not think there was other cause for him wishing to send a message to her. He concluded, however, finally, that he would deceive Zomara with feigned delivery of his message, and return fictitious replies, till he had secured all his gold, and then let him die. What had he to do with Don Altanero's household? He had sense enough to keep within the walls of his prison, where he was king.

Barnabas, accordingly, returned in a short time to Zomara's cell, with paper and ink, which inspired some confidence in Zomara, but not enough to allow him to sign his name, or even Isabel's, to the missive he indited forthwith. But, as might be inferred, Barnabas kept the letter long enough to make himself acquainted with its contents, in order that he might frame a verbal answer, and extort more money by continuing the correspondence.

Zomara, however, was suspicious that his message had not been delivered; but he expressed not his suspicions, but next, after a lapse of a few weeks, bribed the jailer to allow him to look from the barred window of the hall, whence, as Barnabas declared, the mansion of Altanero could be distinctly seen, though at the distance of half a league, and where even a female form might be seen walking sadly toward the cliff overhanging the sea—Isabel! But to this Barnabas would not accede, though Zomara offered him the wealth of the Indies, until he consented to be collared and manacled for perfect security. Zomara reluctantly consented to this; for he knew that when once ironed, he was fettered forever; but what price would he not pay to behold Isabel, fond and faithful Isabel, during the tedious hours of his banishment and incarceration?

And Barnabas, to secure Zomara, whom he feared, would willingly have acceded to almost any request.

Barnabas, too, as might be supposed, kept an intent eye on Zomara's every motion, look and expression, when, having climbed a ladder to the window, he stared at the mansion of Altanero, and sighed again and again, and suddenly started, pressed his face to the bars, and looked with such intensity that seemed to force his eyes from their sockets. Was he insane? Was he a pirate? Why should he love Isabel?

But Barnabas was unmoved by anything else than gold. Pity and compassion were as foreign to him as Sirius. In vain Zomara pleaded with him; in vain he submitted to every inhumanity and brutality to appease his savage whims and humors; to nothing would he yield but gold, and that was a scarce commodity with Zomara, and he husbanded it with the caution of his life. If Barnabas had not been such a coward, possibly he would have searched every stitch of Zomara's clothing, would have torn out every stone in the walls of his cell to obtain any and all moneys secreted there; but he was a coward at heart, as every brutal tyrant is; and besides, he knew it was but a matter of time, till he became possessed of all Zomara might have, while he received his monthly salary for supporting and guarding the crazy prisoner.

Thus matters continued for a period, which brings us up to the time of Isabel's yielding to the suit of Alvaro, her betrothal, and at length to the very day on which the marriage was to be consummated.

On this day, Zomara, becoming very impatient, as the day of his deliverance, as he hoped, drew near, drew out from its hiding place his last piece of gold, and gave it to Barnabas to carry to Isabel another assurance of his devotion to her, while enduring the most excruciating of torments and tortures at being within sight of her, but separated from her by the bar of a dungeon and the ban of his sovereign. But as the events of this day have an especial interest in this story, they may be given more fully and in detail.

XX.

HA! ha!—chuckled Barnabas, as he returned into the hall, after committing Zomara's letter to the flames, having first read it and concocted an answer to suit himself,—Ha! ha! a gallus cove is he! a jolly pirate! But it's a sweet sound when gold clinks with a jailer's key. Well, he got it easy—a gallus pirate! And who would not rob a robber? But did ever I see such a crazy cove in love? Why, he'd stare from the window of this prison at old Altanero's moping girl till he'd go blind! But love's a gallus cove, he is; would sell his soul for the sight of a wench's petticoat half a league off! But love's a fool, he is, and a gallus fool, if he thinks this key will turn, except for gold; and bear her scraps of scribbled paper, except for gold! Ha! ha! bear the scraps of paper to the fire and pocket the gold! What! need a jailer-king be a fool and a clown, to meddle with a nobleman's affairs—for a few pence have a broken crown—and all for a love-sick, crazy pirate in a dungeon!

Soliloquizing thus, or rather to that effect, he went on humming a rude tune to which these ideas, if not words, arranged themselves in his mind—

> Ha! a jailer-king, let me dance and sing!
> For the sceptre I hold,
> Fills my coffers with gold,—
> Hurra! for the jailer-king!

He then unlocked the door of Zomara's cell, and gave him—as he declared—Isabel's reply to his message.

But said she nothing of love? And did she not give you a letter—a token—a word?—asked Zomara, in a sad and plaintive tone, looking, the while, with a vacant stare at the wall of the cell, rather than in the direction of his question.

She said you were a crazy pirate,—answered Barnabas, prefacing his reply with his derisive ejaculatory laugh,—she said you were a crazy pirate, and gave me a cuff for you, which,—suiting the action to the word,—take you now, with interest.

Wretch, you lie!—exclaimed Zomara, rising with more anger, indignation, and excitement, than he had exhibited for many months.—Wretch, you lie!—Come within the circle of these manacles, and your brains will spatter these prison walls! You gave her not my letter; she has not seen my blood-written words; she did not call me pirate; your own savage heart has conjured up this brutal message!

Go on! my gallus cove!—cried out Barnabas, unmoved by the agony he had subjected his prisoner to, but stung to the quick by the imputation of lying to him, a defamation of character he must not submit to.—Go on! rant! gall your limbs with your irons! hack your voice with bellowing! —then back to your cell to a dinner of straw, for nothing else shall you eat to-day, except your filthy bed!—Call me a liar? Ha! a gallus cove, are you! She not only called you a liar, but added, tell the fool that to-day Alvaro, the noble, rich and handsome, bears me to his home a willing, joyous bride!—Call me a liar? Heard you not the bells at break of day—heard you not their iron tongues peal out the merry wedding chimes?

This taunt, a lie though he believed it, was nevertheless too terrible to Zomara not to affect him seriously. He became calm immediately; sank from wild excitement, allied to fury, to reflection sad; nay, overwhelming. His limbs began to tremble, and a cold clammy sweat to ooze from his skin.

Mock me not,—at length the tortured man said, in a dignified, determined tone, that bore the impress of truth and power to the heart of even the brutal, petty tyrant Barnabas,—I may not be what I appear.—Cast on shore with the wreck of a pirate's vessel, and picked up a pirate; carried to the dungeon and confined as a pirate, yet I may not be a pirate; manacled and maltreated as a pirate; yet I may not be one, for all that; no, nor crazy, as the judge determined, and confined me here. Beware, then, how you taunt me. Now give me her message aright, if sent she any, if, villain as I know you to be, you were less the villain you appear to be enough to deliver my message.

Perhaps not a pirate,—said Barnabas in amaze, and still feeling the defamation of character,— but submitting as such—carried to this keep as such—fed on musty bread and rotten meat as such —and all this for nigh two years—and not a pirate! Then a fool—a gallus fool, which is seven times worse!—But perhaps I lie—perhaps I taunt you—perhaps I mock you? Would you like to look from the window at the hall and see the flags fluttering for very joy over the houses of Altanero and Borracho? I'll fetch the ladder.

Fairly gloating over the agony his words produced, the brutal jailer left Zomara a few minutes to his own thoughts, while he procured the ladder.

Can this be true?—he asked himself.—No, no; her heart is knit with mine so closely and so surely that death alone can sever us. No, no; I am bold to look again from the window at the walls which hold the pure and faithful Isabel—oh, how these wasted, shackled arms do envy them! But this brutal jailer doubtless has been deceiving me? She may believe me dead!—how terrible the thought. Alas! if my submission to the charge of piracy, nay, to rob the dead of his apparel, and steal the mania of a madman to assert a crazy pirate's claim to clemency, to save my life, and be in Spain near Isabel, should prove my death—aye, worse than death a thousand fold—within the sight of Isabel, almost within my call, to see her carried to the altar, and to wed my murderer, as she and all must deem him! Heard I not her voice as I fell from the cliff? Saw she not the murderer? And can she—Isabel—accept the hand, red with the blood of him, for whom she would have dared the rage of seas, the wrath of parents thwarted, and shared an exile's shame and poverty? No! no! it cannot be! This jailer does but mock me. For what cares he for ought I love? Was it not but yesterday, when my tamed spider, at my call, crept in to cheer me in my solitude, that he trod my fellow-prisoner under foot, laughing the while like a demon—"Ha! a gallus bloated cove!"—Oh, that I could have brained the monster on the spot!

About the instant Zomara reached this vindictive point, Barnabas returned with a ladder, and placed it against the wall of the prison, below the window looking toward Altanero's mansion—led Zomara into the hall, and bade the tortured prisoner ascend.

Perhaps I mock you?—said he again, with his brutal sneer.—There, take the ladder, and gaze until your eyes weep tears of blood.

Zomara, despite his determination, trembled as he rested on the first round of the ladder.

Perhaps I lie? Ha! ha! a gallus cove afraid to look at his sweetheart. Go up, go up, my gallus cove.

Zomara slowly climbed to a point whence he could look through the window, and his heart grew sick and faint as he saw the evidences of the truth of Barnabas' words before him.

It is as he has said,—he sighed to himself.—I see the flags, the bustle of the servants, and the carriages of the nobility of Grenada. But on the terrace, whence I fell,—so his sad thoughts wandered as his eyes rested on the cliff in the garden,—and where I have often seen a female form appear, deeply clad in the sables of woe, and stand as if she gazed, with wistful looks, upon the sea that swallowed all she loved,—so I fondly dreamed,—I now see nobody! But, hold!—is that a gleam of sunlight from the waves?—No, it is a form in robes of white!—Oh, look! she hurls herself into the sea! No! no! my brain is reeling! Help! help!

Zomara staggered down several rounds of the ladder, his strength relaxing with every round, till, reaching the second or third round from the floor, he was completely exhausted, and sank heavily to the floor.

It was Isabel, indeed, whom he had seen. Before going to the cathedral, where the ceremony of her marriage was to be performed, she had stolen away from Teresa and other attendants, and walked alone to the cliff to muse and mourn once more over the death of Zomara—once more to feel with the entirety of her passion, its free outpouring for the loved and the lost—once more to be Isabel, the betrothed of Zomara, and free as the universe in the expression of her expanding affection; and forever after to be the wife of Alvaro, the slave of duty, and the meek, contracted point of passive obedience to a self not her own.

Ah, could Isabel have known that Zomara saw her at that very instant and divined her inmost thought! Think of it! was situation ever more strange and sad than theirs?

But let us go back to heart-broken Zomara, lying at the foot of the ladder, exhausted, and gasping for breath, as if with the last throes of expiring strength.

Welcome, death!—said he, faintly, clutching at his iron collar, to which his wrists were chained, as if to free his neck from that which was choking him.

Ha! a gallus strangled cove!—roared out the demoniac Barnabas.—Perhaps I lie? Perhaps I mock you? eh?

One breath of air! then let me die in peace!—sadly said the sinking soldier.—Unlock this iron band!

Zomara was evidently dying, strangled by his collar apparently, but in reality by the sinking of his heart within him from the terrible shock he had just experienced. Barnabas looked upon him with mingled feelings of satisfied revenge, atoned honor, and devilish delight. Soon, however, his controlling avarice took possession of him. He was acquiring gold by keeping and guarding the crazy pirate, and his revenue must not be cut off. There was a doubt, moreover, that entered his mind, that Zomara was, as he declared a little while before, not a pirate. His interest in Isabel was too deep and terrible to be the caprice or delusion of a crazy man. He might be able to ransom himself, if he would only recover and declare himself.

Ha! ha! there may be gold in this carcass yet!—thought the jailer, as he stooped and unlocked the collar, and liberated Zomara's neck.

Zomara slowly recovered, and as he did so, Barnabas resumed his taunts and mockery.

Ha! a throttled cove! But perhaps I lie?

Zomara, however, recovered more rapidly than Barnabas imagined. Feeling himself comparatively free, the first idea that suggested itself was to make use of his freedom, make a desperate effort to overcome Barnabas, escape from the dungeon, and interrupt, again, the marriage of Isabel with Alvaro; for he was convinced she was forced by circumstances, and not by inclination, to wear the white robes he had seen from the window. It was a daring attempt to make; to achieve the most opportune victory of his life; and to fail, to lose his life, most probably; but what was death to him in his situation—not even a thought. Collecting his strength, accordingly, and concentrating,

cautiously, his entire being to one intent, he watched, with a lurking but intensely keen eye, for an opportunity when Barnabas would be off his guard. The moment soon arrived. Barnabas turned from Zomara and stooped to pick up the great key of the dungeon, which had been dropped during the excitement incident to relieving his strangled prisoner. One spring, like a hungry tiger's, and Zomara was on the back of Barnabas, his hands clutching about his neck, and bearing him to the floor with his weight! The advantage gained was decisive. The struggle was long; but Zomara clung to the throat of the jailer, and kept his weight as much as possible on his shoulders; and, at length, he held him fast beneath him, pinioned to the floor with his knees between his shoulders, and kept his hold on the throttle till all signs of life ceased. Zomara then relaxed his hold of the throat cautiously, took up the heavy key with his right hand, and raised it high above the jailer's head, intending to bring it down with all his force and dash out the brains of his opponent.

But the effort was too exhausting to the enervated prisoner, already worn out by the continued struggle. He felt for an instant the exhilarating joy of victory, hailed the key that was about to descend and crash through the skull of Barnabas as the key of his deliverance; but his senses, the next instant, began to swim, and his eye lost the directing control of his hand; the key dropped harmless by the side of the victim's head, and the fainting prisoner fell forward senseless!

Barnabas in a short time recovered his breath, and disengaged himself from the superincumbent Zomara.

Ha! a crazy gallus cove! with a grip like a vise!—began his thoughts, as he crawled from under Zomara, and rose to his feet,—I thought I was gone. 'Tis a long time since I've thought of my mother, but I saw her even now. She was in her old, red gown, and was shedding tears over my coffin! But the jailer-king's not dead yet!—What! the gallus cove still kicks?—observing signs of returning life in Zomara.—Ha! ha! I'll collar him again—a second time I will not incur this danger.

Thinking which, Barnabas secured the collar about Zomara's neck, and watched his recovery with more interest than before, but with the same diabolical taunts.

Now, back to your cell!—at length he said, when he thought Zomara was recovered sufficiently to walk.—Back to your cell! But perhaps I mock you?

No; you do not mock me,—responded Zomara, despairingly.—Take me back to my cell; and when I die—ah, it will not be long till that blessed moment arrives—write on the door of my tomb, ZOMARA, OF CASTILE, for I am he!

Zomara, of Castile!—repeated the astonished Barnabas. Why,—said he to himself,—this is a gallus prize! The king offers a thousand gold doubloons for Zomara's head! Ha! the gallus traitor—the gallus banished man! A prize! A thousand gold doubloons! I knew he was no pirate! I said he was not crazy! Ha! the gallus rogue, to play his part so well!

Yes, jailer, I am Zomara, of Castile,—continued the despairing man. — Now listen; Altanero's daughter, Isabel, is betrothed to me. She believes me dead, and is forced to marry Alvaro. Release me, and whatever reward you may ask from my father's estate shall be yours.

Ha! ha! a bribing cove!—replied Barnabas, resuming his taunting tone.—No, no; a gallus bird in the hand's worth two in the bush.

Zomara, then, at a loss to know with what thing of direct and present value he could move the heart of the avaricious wretch, bethought him of the ring he had secreted in the lining of his garment when he was first put in confinement, and immediately tore it out, and held it before the greedy eyes of his keeper.

Here is a ring,—said he,—in which our names are inscribed. For nearly two years it has been concealed in these poor rags. Show it to-day to Isabel, before her marriage, and say to her that Zomara still lives, and not only the ring, but a fortune for life, will be yours.

A ring!—exclaimed Barnabas, snatching it from Zomara's hand.—I'll go. Your name is in it, is it? Ha! ha! But perhaps I mock you? Per-

haps I lie? Ha! you gallus traitor, this proof of your presence in Spain to-day will lay your head upon the block, and put a thousand gold doubloons in my pocket! Ha! a gallus ring!

Then go, accursed villain, to the king!—said Zomara, impatiently, and aroused to wrath at the suggestion of the injustice of the sentence he was submitting to.—Say to him, Zomara, of Castile, is in your cell. Say, too, he longs for death, by the command of the king for whom he has risked his life on deck and field in fierce engagement, but not by the villainy of a brutal, avaricious jailer. Send me back to my cell.

And Barnabas, muttering to himself, in the fullness of his joy at the unexpected prize that had fallen into his hands, led Zomara to his cell, and turned the key on him.

Ha! a gallus banished cove! One thousand gold doubloons!

> Ha! a jailer-king, let me dance and sing!
> For the sceptre I hold,
> Fills my coffers with gold,—
> Hurra! for the jailer-king!

XXI.

EXCEPTING Zomara and Barnabas, all the personages introduced in this story were found beneath the roof of Altanero's mansion on the morning of the day on which the nuptials of Isabel and Alvaro were to be solemnized. The assemblage was remarkable for various and diverse thoughts and feelings—though, in truth, what half a score or more of persons were ever gathered together, if their several histories of the heart were revealed, of whom this remark could not be applied as well?

Altanero, divided between love and pride, looked careworn and haggard. The past ten months had added as many years to his being, if the furrows of anxiety and the silvery hairs of mental misery stand for aught in the annals of time. He loved Isabel dearly, and with a tenderness approaching childishness, as he witnessed her melancholy and her gradual sinking from an individuality of intense passion and noble aspirations into a passive puppet of despair. He would have yielded gladly to her preference for Zomara over Alvaro, had he known Zomara still lived; but, Zomara dead, he was heart-broken to see her cling with such pertinacity to his memory, till, her vitality absorbed, she seemed a fitting bride for a ghost. On the other hand, he was proud of the lineage of the Altaneros, continued for centuries, one of the noblest families of Grenada; and he esteemed it the great aim and object of his life to extend the line still further down the stream of time. Through Isabel was his only hope. And Zomara dead, the only means that circumstances presented was the suit of Alvaro, unexceptionable to him in every particular, nay, eminently fitting in every respect. He could reason himself very readily, moreover, into the belief that marriage, with such an estimable nobleman as Alvaro, would soon restore a healthy tone to her mind and body.

The new relationship she would encounter in married life, and the new forces excited into activity within her, which would annul or divert the forces then ruling her to her ruin, would make such a change in her for the better, that she must necessarily be a happier being. As long as he confined himself to contemplation and reason, he was convinced and determined to effect this marriage for Isabel's own sake, as well as his own, and the inherited interests of the family name. He saw more in the union, too, than happiness and continuance; he saw wealth in a glittering pile of gold, surrounded with a lustrous halo, in the glamour of which Melancholy danced, Misery mocked itself, and Woe, wreathed with roses, and radiant with smiles, presided like a queen, in the stead of Happiness. But to execute his conviction and will—there lay the harrow that, scoring his brow, tore through the subsoil of his sensibility with remorseless tine! When he looked upon Isabel, pale and wan, poor, heart-broken Isabel—a blighted corolla of a lovely flower, delicate and fragile as substance could exist and retain shape and form; he even feared to tremble in its presence, lest the slightest agitation would stir it from the stem and

separate it into flake-like petals, to fall, to scatter, and pave the way for the noiseless foot of Death, daintily tripping to his lonely, secluded dell.

In a sad and wavering reverie, accordingly, must you see Altanero on the morning of Isabel's wedding day; and when you learn that, when all was excitement and bustle about the house, he glided into her apartment to embrace her with the fullness of his feeling for her, and crave her forgiveness if he urged her to a fate that might prove in the slightest degree unhappy to her, you will understand the abject and depressing dismay that seized him when he found her gone! You will understand why his head swam and the poise of his eye was lost; why he felt faint, and staggered to the window for a breath of fresh and revivifying air; and when he recovered from the shock, and looking out, beheld Isabel on the cliff, a snow-white semblance of Sorrow gazing sadly into the illimitable sea, telling its story of woe and despair with a tongue that roared in the ear of the soul with its very silence, you will understand why the old man, the fond father, buried his face in his hands, and wept like a lost and lonely child.

How different the feelings of Borracho, the father of Alvaro! Bacchus predominant, the wealthy and jovial old Don was in glorious glee. He joked, and laughed, and sang. And whatever he did, it was with that impetuosity of his nature, which, inherited by Alvaro, and directed into philosophy instead of high living and good fellowship, made him the daring, doubting and dangerous man that he was. The old Don recognized this in his son as his own impulse, for, in spite of him, he was ever on the outskirts of philosophy, but had not the learning of his son to enter the vast field, and thoroughly comprehend his son or his reasonings. However, as he recognized the impulse or tendency as his own, and was satisfied with himself, if ever mortal was, he had full trust and confidence in Alvaro, was proud of him, and was firmly convinced he would be an intellectual hero of the family, as many of his ancestors had been military and political heroes before him. But the old Don, Borracho, was high toned with respect to what he considered the honor of a nobleman, and this gave him more concern with respect to Alvaro than anything else. He was not altogether satisfied that his son was entirely clear from the imputation of treachery toward Zomara, if, indeed, he was not implicated in his murder, if that were a fact; but the suspicion grew faint as time wore on, and every evidence seemed to exonerate rather than implicate Alvaro in anything dishonorable, and Borracho, instead of loathing and, if possible, disinheriting his son, loved and admired him with the generous and confiding affection of a father, open, frank, generous and jovial in his nature to a fault. On the morning of the day in consideration, he had turned over to Alvaro the revenues of several estates in Grenada, which would furnish him with a bountiful competence for himself and wife and children, if Heaven should bless the union with a perpetuation of life, —the assurance, above all others, that marriages are made in Heaven. He insisted, however, that Alvaro should make his home in the halls of his ancestors, where the presence of Isabel, the pure and lovely Isabel, filling the measure of his son's happiness, by his side, would, in a measure, fill the vacancy occasioned by the death of Alvaro's mother, a woman of queenly form, noble instincts, and holy love, a beloved wife, who sacrificed her existence in the terrible throes that ushered Alvaro into being.

But hear Borracho laugh and sing in the hall of Altanero!—wouldst think he ever buried a beloved wife? wouldst think he ever thought of her kindly, sadly, and with tears of regret from the heart? wouldst think, but an hour ago, he had recited to Alvaro the worth and virtue of his mother, and pointed to her portrait on the wall with a trembling finger, saying, sadly,— Your mother, my son; like unto her be Isabel; no greater wish for your earthly happiness can I utter!

No; such mirth and such misery seem incompatible; but below the most boisterous laugh, and beneath the most derogatory jest with respect to marriage, there was a sepulchre of sorrow wherein the memory of the loved and the lamented lay enshrined forever; as beneath the floral mound, where mercenary bees exchange the love missives of amorous flowers for a tiny tribute of golden honey, and where butterflies sport on gaily decked wing, as false and as fickle as the fashion of an hour may be—as beneath this glare of floral beauty, honeyed sweetness, and fickle fancy, a grave may lie wherein the form of manly worth, or womanly virtue, moulders away, loses shape and texture, and lapses surely into indistinguishable clay. Yes; Borracho did feel and could forget, and the feeling was not the less deep and true for all that; for the forgetfulness was only on the surface, where the unaided eye could behold it and give it undue importance; while memory and feeling lay concealed within, too sacred for the vulgar gaze, too tender for the heartless shocks of an unfeeling world, and too little dreamed of to be of any significance.

Alvaro paced up and down the hall. To all appearances, and the circumstances considered, he was meditating over his approaching nuptials.

Heigho! have you lost your discourse?—said Quesada, twittingly, to him, as he approached him in his moody wandering.—That aphasia should be a sequela of love is not set down in the books. But your case is well marked and authentic.

Transitory aphasia may,—replied Alvaro, awakening from his reverie sufficiently to understand Quesada's question, but continuing his walking to and fro.

I grant you,—said Quesada, as Alvaro approached again,—that transitory aphasia does exist, but never in wives, especially, my morose friend, when husbands are moody without cause; and never as a sequence of love, if I have read my books aright. You have observed it during convalescence from severe attacks of fever, have you not?

Occasionally—rarely,—answered Alvaro, turning away.

When it was owing to cerebral congestion?—continued Quesada.

Possibly,—replied Alvaro.

But not to love?—said the jocular old doctor, and not without point.

No,—and down the hall went Alvaro again.

You are satisfied, too,—resumed Quesada, as his victim approached,—that the faculty of speech, or expressing thought thereby, lies not in the posterior portion of the third frontal convolution of the brain, mainly on the sinister aspect?

Yes; for experience disproves the theory.

True; but you will admit that aphasia, with hemiplegia on the right side, is the most common form.

Well, yes; but what then?—asked Alvaro, a little impatiently.

Have you ever known it to result before from the action of the heart, on the eve of matrimony?

Never before,—replied Alvaro; adding, with possibly too much severity,—as I have never known its opposite, garrulity, to issue with such volubility on the subject of matrimony—

From such an old and hard-hearted bachelor,—added Quesada, when Alvaro seemed to hesitate for lack of a mild and appropriate phrase.

As you like it,—concluded Alvaro, and continued his walk.

Alvaro's meditations, however, were disturbed by Quesada's catechising; the continuity of his reverie was broken, and on his return he sat down by his friend's side, begged his pardon for his rudeness, and discoursed with him as pleasantly on any subject broached as Quesada could desire, till the time for going to the cathedral should arrive.

With this view of Alvaro's exterior, let us now take a look at his interior, if it be but a glance.

During the past night, on three occasions, he heard a voice cry out to him—Beware! Beware!

There was not so much to him in the import of the mysterious speech, as there was in the tone. There was something familiar about it that, at the first sound, sent a shudder through him. And though thrice only he heard the warning, it haunted him continually, and rang in his ears with a reverberation that threatened to echo through his very existence. It was the voice of the beloved of his early manhood—the voice of a poor, confiding girl betrayed by him in an evil hour! But whence came it?—he asked himself a thousand times. Distance and years had buried her from sight and hearing. Was she not dead, as reported, years ago, to his emissaries, sent with money without stint for

her support? At any rate, how could she know him as Alvaro, when she heard and knew none other than Rodrigo? She was in Catalonia and he in Grenada. Surely, thought he, the dead has not come to life; Rodrigo is known only to Alvaro; and Catalonia is still many, many leagues away from Grenada. Could it be the voice of conscience crying within, with such distinctness that the air without seemed responsive thereto? Has remorse then, too, a tongue as well as a corroding tooth? But in vain could he reason an internal source for the sound. The reality forced itself upon him, but the mystery still remained unsolved; where was the person? It was constant with him, this series of questions and doubts and surmises, through the night; followed him to Altanero's, and ceased not till Quesada's persistent inquiries forced his thoughts into other channels, and gave to him at least the happy semblance of a man about to wed the fairest and the worthiest woman in Grenada.

Lady Mariana, her thoughts turning of late years almost altogether to religion, passed the greater portion of the morning in seclusion and prayer. She was happy at the thought of Isabel's marriage with Alvaro; for, though she knew him to be skeptical on every tenet of her creed, yet she doubted not her ability to persuade him to implicit faith in due time—at all events, it afforded her the only relaxation from her monotonous prayer to discuss religion with him, who was condescending enough to humor her in her whims, oppose, to incite her to discussion, and yield, to gratify her vanity, as he saw she required it.

Belonging to the same type, as mother and daughter should, were Lady Mariana and Isabel; both inclined to contemplation, introspection, and melancholy; but Isabel, receiving the tender and affectionate heart of her father, lapsed into the melancholy of love, while her mother's tendencies were predominantly toward religion.

But Isabel, when she yielded to the suit of Alvaro, passed from melancholy to the passive indifference of despair, and the cold, plastic obedience of duty. For several days past she had even twitted love as the bearer of sorrow, and commended duty as the only true road to happiness. With her mother's spirit of conversion, too, she would argue with Teresa, and became provoked at her for asserting that neither love nor religion were subject to reason or argument, but lived by faith and constancy. She went even further: she rebuked Teresa for growing cold toward her, for avoiding her presence, and even of ingratitude to her. Ah, little did she suspect the cause that estranged her bosom friend and confidante from her! Little did she dream of the abyss that was widening between them—a fatal chasm for both, the instant one became the wife of Alvaro, and the other, herself.—She shuddered at the logic that led to the thought, long before her ideas reached the dreadful juncture of eternal shame.

The indifference of Isabel, however, was assumed, not real. Natures that ages have required to develop, are not changed wholly without a like lapse of time. Her second nature was worn like a cloak, and illy worn; for in her stealing away to the solitude of the cliff, and gazing into the sea with that sadness which, when born, never dies, the garb of indifference to love fell from her shoulders, and revealed the Maid of Melancholy, with all the distinctness as when, holding the dagger of Zomara in her hand and about to plunge it into her bosom, the apparition of Zomara rose before her, and solved the enigma of the symbols, and she, kissing the dagger with rapture, instead of killing herself with it, sank into a chair in the very ecstacy of love.

A look, now, into the heart of Teresa. For years she had loved Alvaro with the entirety of her warm and affectionate nature; for years she had borne the woe of her betrayal and desertion with uncomplaining patience and forbearance, under the most agonizing tortures; for years she had stood near him, in the guise of Isabel's governess, a guardian who would sacrifice herself to any aim or ambition he might have, but not to love; to her only did his heart belong, by right of conquest, years ago; by virtue of unnumbered vows treasured in her memory, with the accent of love with which they were uttered still imprinted on them; and, above all, by the existence of a son,

whom she had borne to him in the cold and unfeeling seclusion and shame of a strange town, amid strange people, and whom she had reared in the same seclusion, till the likeness of the father was indubitably and incontestibly Alvaro's, to be shown in proof of her assertions any time she saw fit to declare them. But she knew the haughty nature of the nobleman, Alvaro; she knew the awful chasm between him and her lowly being; she knew, moreover, the taint of Moorish blood in her veins, that would separate him from her as widely as rank and fortune; she knew that he would spurn her from his side like a dog or a loathsome leprosy the instant she would reveal herself, let alone claim him as her husband, and trample law and justice under foot, till he had hunted her and her darling boy to death as impostors; she knew all this with the sagacity of an observing, calculating and deeply-wronged woman; and one thing more: she must abide her time, when circumstances, like an overwhelming avalanche, are at her back to roll down and crush all opposition, if even Alvaro and herself and child share the general ruin.

For nearly two years she had fostered Isabel's love for Zomara, though it wrung her very soul to witness the agony the forlorn devotee of love endured in memory of the daring soldier murdered by Alvaro, as she alone and the circumstances could bear witness; for Isabel's many virtues and noble nature had endeared her to her as a second self, but not as another Alvaro. But when Isabel, however compulsory the circumstances, abandoned the ghost, whom she had hugged to her bosom so long and so tenderly, and yielded to Alvaro's suit, that instant another passion held joint sway with love in Teresa's breast—jealousy; deep, daring, and deadly jealousy, that soon grew familiar with thoughts of daggers directed in the dark at sleeping innocence, to be declared on the morrow the effect of despair! of deadly draughts and poisoned potions in the nuptial wine! of suffocating pillows! of charcoal embers, deepening sleep, down, down to death! and such like dark and terrible intents, that only the monsters of Jealousy and Mammon can conjure up.

Ah, when we recur to Isabel chiding Teresa for her seeming coldness toward her, and her unaccountable estrangement, we must tremble to see her on the brink of destruction, tripping along with slight concern on the edge of a precipice, which the darkness of trust and intimacy of years renders unseen and unsuspected.

And Nona, and Martin, and Pedro, must not be forgotten in this general review of the personages of this story under the roof of Altanero's house before the wedding party set out, with all the pomp and array of nobility, for the grand old cathedral, where the ceremony was to be performed.

Nona has grown no younger, nor comelier, nor less rheumatic; on the contrary, the disappearance of several teeth brought her chin and nose into closer proximity, and a greater intimacy than they had ever before enjoyed; the crow-foot of time had been imprinted with greater distinctness on the corners of her eyes; and the sparrows of the neighborhood had not lacked for grizzled combings from her head wherewith to weave and thatch their nests together. So much for her increased age; which will do, too, for her decreased comeliness; and for her rheumatism, suffice it that it had settled principally in one finger, stiffened it into a rigidity that thrust it perversely into and against everything, even into Martin's ears and against Pedro's fiery nose; and, curiously enough, the finger afflicted was the one upon which an engagement ring is generally worn, so it looked as if the old maid had gotten into a chronic habit of holding it out in expectation of such a symbol, till the finger naturally stiffened in that position : the suggestion, at all events, is irresistible.

Martin has not grown a day older in appearance; still gets drunk when he has an opportunity, has a witty rencounter with Dr. Quesada now and then, filches whatever he can from Pedro, and still loves Nona to keep even with Pedro, and give color to the rakish jokes he plays on the solemn, sanctimonious expounder of the philosophic dogma, that a woman's a woman the wide world over.

Pedro, however, has grown older, if Martin has not; he has grown thinner in flesh, moreover, if that were possible; but what he has lost in body he has gained in nose: not to make an odious comparison, but really he reminded one of, if he did not in fact resemble, a bean-pole with a boiled lobster tacked near the top—about as far from the ground as the red nose in question. And as his nose grew in proportions and heightened in color, he became more solemn and severely sanctimonious in his deportment. He even evinced choler when Quesada intimated, as a corollary to his Bardolphian nose, a hob-nailed liver, the effect of spiritual acquaintance and absorption. He exhibited, moreover, a faint spirit of chivalry when Quesada intimated that if Nona could not wear rings on her fingers, and particularly on that stiff one, she could wear them around her eyeballs in evidence of her age and fatty degeneration of her tissues. He even went so far as to accuse Quesada of quackery in putting Nona on a lemon-juice treatment for her rheumatism, which, of course, did her rheumatism no good, and only soured her temper the more.

XXII.

NOTHING of any moment happened on the way to the cathedral. To all external appearances the occasion was one of great rejoicing. The people of the town stood in groups on the pavements, or thronged the windows of the houses in front of which the procession passed, and wondered at the justice of Heaven in bestowing such rare blessings and bounties on some, and depriving others of even the necessaries of life. Ah, little they thought that beneath the show and tinsel of that parade, there were crime and woe; hearts wrung with anguish, and minds burdened with remorse, or charred into coals, to be fired only by jealousy, that darkest and deadliest of passions! Little they thought that the altar of Hymen, beneath its garland of flowers, was a bloody block, upon which the pure and innocent were to be immolated in atonement for the vice and crime of others! Yet, such is the world and its rendition in all ages; an outer hull and an inner kernel, and oh, how sadly different at times!

The bridal party entered the cathedral and proceeded up the aisle in solemn state.

No; Isabel nor faltered nor trembled. Determination bore her up more than her father's arm, on which she hung. A reproving look she even gave Teresa, who accompanied her, deeply veiled, and clad in vestments indicating rather woe than happiness, and preserving an austere, unusual, and unaccountable silence, unless it were from grief at the approach of separation from her beloved charge.

Doubt me not, Teresa,—she whispered to her,—Alvaro shall not engross my care and affection, that my devoted friend and companion of years shall be slighted or forgotten. My home shall be yours, to share its joys and sorrows, as of old. Come, kiss me, dear, devoted friend.

But Teresa turned away, and answered not. It had been a source of extreme anxiety to avoid discovery by Alvaro during the time she had been with Isabel, and as long as she was confined to the house, under the assumed name of Teresa, and in the guise of a matronly governess, this was comparatively easy; but now her difficulties were multiplied a thousand fold, and under the mask of sorrow only was she able to avoid detection. And how far more befitting were silence and gloom to her than speech and sunshine? She turned away and answered not, for the double reason that jealousy could not answer such tender love, and a deep and dire intent could not at that instant discover itself.

But what were Alvaro's thoughts, you ask, as he approached the altar, and knelt by the side of Isabel, and awaited the holy utterance of the priest which would declare vice and virtue indissolubly united forever?

Nor time, nor place, nor occasion, possessed wholly his mind. In ready response to any and all impressions received through his acute senses, it rolled about and reviewed one thing after another with rare rapidity and kaleidoscopic variety.

The fullness and the profundity of the reverberation in the vault above—leading to waves of sound—waves to the sea—and the ocean to Zomara—and Zomara to guilt—and guilt to punishment!

The mellow light in the vast hall, and the sunshine streaming through the stained and illumined windows in faint and parti-colored streaks—leading to thoughts and theories of light—to the spectral analysis—and spectral to delusion—and delusion to the spectre of Zomara, which possessed the mind of Isabel—and his own soul!

Then came, alternate with the eye, an impression through the ear. The deep, sonorous tones of the organ rolled in majestic waves through the grand old cathedral, and beat back against the walls, and commingled, till the air was a very surge of sound, with a chant or intonation of a voice now and then rising above, clear and distinct, like a jet of spray. And, soothed by the commingled sounds, his mind lay on the lap of melancholy in subdued and calm slumber, but only for an instant; introspection will not sleep for the guilty—for with thoughts of music came thoughts of harmony, and harmony led to peace, and peace to its opposite, war, and war to blood, and blood—his own chilled in anticipation of the threatened sequence!

Then rose the holy incense, filling the air with its impressive fragrance, and awing the mind with the surfeit of another sense. But thoughts of odors led to flowers, and flowers led to evanescent beauty—and beauty led to Isabel.

And with this last thought, Alvaro raised his eyes, and gazed into the face of Isabel.

He recalled the full, flushed cheek of her girlhood; then came he to contemplation of her wan and saddened features at present; and one remove farther into the future, he saw the grim and ghostly outlines of a skull through the thin gauze of flesh and blood. And he shuddered again as he thought of the terrible crime that concentrated the past, the present, and the future of a noble woman into the brief compass of a glance!

Next, he wondered at his own reflective being, and lapsed into a reverie in contemplation of the action of his mind. And, in his deep abstraction, he heeded not the words of the priest, but on, on he went from one phase to another, till,

44

57

in poetic form, his logic and conclusion ran as follows:

A fiction, a dream,
A poet's theme,—
   Yet such may fall in the scales of the mind
And kick the beam
    To good or evil;
Less, by far,
Can make or mar
   A golden harvest to rustic hind—
    Rain-drop or weevil!

For though the Mind
Is a wizard king,
To draw in the skull his magic ring,
And raise the spirits of water and wind—
   Kelpie, goblin and ghost,—
Aye, and the genii of earth's dark caves,
   And the fiends of fire,—
   A host
Of willing, abject, able slaves,
   To make a deed of their master's desire;
Yet it seldom can rule that little elf,
Itself;
But, with nimble motion,
At the prick of a whim, or the spur of a notion,
Turns it about, with supple joints,
To one or the other cardinal points
   Of the moralist's compass, good or evil,
   God or devil!

But you grow impatient. This analysis of thought in a philosophic mind, at a juncture when you expect an exciting episode and hurried action, is aggravating. I will admit this, and you, in turn, must admit that since action of the body follows action of the mind, to understand fully the former, you must comprehend the latter. Without an inside acquaintance with Alvaro, his actions would be as unintelligible to you as they were to Quesada when he attempted to oppose him with a drawn lancet.

Suffice it, then, that the ceremony of marriage had so far progressed that the priest officiating, an archbishop in full canonicals, and attended with all the majesty and pomp and sacred circumstance of his high and holy office, had reached that important and impressive point, when, addressing the assembled people, in tones inspiring duty and courage, he said aloud—

If any there be who can show just cause why this man and woman may not lawfully be joined together in holy matrimony, I require and charge him, as he shall answer at the judgment day, when the secrets of all hearts are disclosed, now to speak, or else hereafter forever to hold his peace. For be assured, that if any are joined together otherwise than as God's Holy Word doth allow, their marriage is not lawful.

A moment of impressive silence followed this stern and significant declaration.

The priest was about to resume, when Teresa, casting aside her veil, and displaying a face set with desperation and despair, stepped boldly forward.

There is one here, most holy man of God, whose desolated heart is written over and over with burning, damning proofs which bar the consummation of those marriage vows!

Teresa uttered this with a distinctness, a deliberation, and an emphasis, which, as its import was determined, created a horror that was appalling, and an amaze that lapsed into awe.

Protect us, Gracious Lady!—exclaimed Lady Mariana, the first to regain her speech, and use it in an appeal to the Virgin,—what can my daughter's guide and governess, at this late hour, object against her marriage?

Alvaro's back, as he knelt by the side of Isabel, was turned toward Teresa when she interrupted the ceremony with her speech, the purport of which was so terrible to all. He saw her not. But the voice that had haunted him for years, and had called out to him in the night to Beware! was the voice he heard. He knew its source; and, as if paralyzed by its tone, remained in his humble posture as motionless as a statue of stone.

Joanna Mauritan, of Catalonia, asserts her rights,—continued Teresa, her face flushing, and her eyes flashing fire.—Alvaro is her husband in the light of truth and by the laws of Heaven; for he, a lover came, with fair, false face and name, and won her pure and trusting heart; and then, more harsh and cruel than the beasts of the desert, who grow milder when their dams and sucklings pass, this proud, relentless man, with sneer and scoff, did spurn his child, and cast away to shame the mother, who, in secret pain, without complaint, had borne his son—the offspring of her trust and his deceit!

As Teresa continued, horror and dismay increased, and all eyes were turned toward Alvaro, who still remained on his knees.

I pray you, father,—at length, he said, rising, and addressing the archbishop in a confident tone, while a smile of assurance and satire played on his complacent countenance,—I pray you, father, heed not words that rush so madly forth from one who owns herself unfit to stand within this church,—much less to bar these sacraments. She is a Moor, also, the constant enemy of Spain's nobility, unless it bears the taint of heathen sires.

I scorn to mark the sneer that ill becomes a man,—as sternly added Teresa; then, as she felt the taunt in Alvaro's allusion to her Moorish blood, with even more earnestness than before, she continued, looking defiantly at Alvaro, and with a fierceness that plainly showed her impetuous passion in all its force had shifted into hatred and revenge.—There are black taints of blood, however, which do not come from descent; for see that hand, extended there in solemn form with pledge and emblem of eternal love,—it is foul with human blood! that hand, just joined in soft caress with purity, has taken the life of man—the life of Zomara, of Castile!

Alvaro murder Zomara!—exclaimed Isabel, as if her comprehension was too slight to take down at a gulp the immensity of the horror as expressed by Teresa.

Yes, my lady, Alvaro murdered Zomara!—replied Teresa; then fixing her eyes as if she saw the tragedy enacted before her, she continued,—I now see Alvaro, with red and reeking sword yet drawn, as he, by conscience driven, fled the sight of man! I now see Zomara as he, wounded, fell into the sea, while thunders rolled, and angry, lashing waves, beating against the rocks, tossed lives like toys into eternity!

Such was the night,—said Altanero, who had approached Isabel with fond solicitude, and now stood by her side, recalling the scene of the most exciting day of his family's history, and seeking to comprehend the circumstances and weigh their import and importance,—such was the night of that dark day, on which their swords were drawn for Isabel! Revenge and jealousy the motives!

The last sentence of Altanero was uttered, not so much as a conclusion as a surmise to himself; but it had the effect of a conclusion and a conviction to all who heard it.

Bermeho stood appalled: his suspicions, facts; his doubts, realities; and what he dreaded most, now bearing down with the overwhelming force of an avalanche to ruin and dishonor! That ruin should result, however, he cared but little; but dishonor and infamy to the proud old Don were worse a hundred-fold than the destruction of all his worldly goods and chattels.

Alas! that our ancient family's lustre,—he sighed aloud,—should end in the darkness of a murderer's grave!

The confidence of Alvaro began to quail. A pallor stole over his face, and the sneer of satire disappeared in a wan and vacant stare. There was a witness to the murder he little suspected! And that witness was witness to another sin or crime—neither word is strong enough to designate the infamy and inhumanity of it—which he believed the grave had swallowed up for years! One accusation of such terrible import, he, perhaps, could have borne and derided into disgrace, with the effrontery, subtlety, and daring courage of his nature; but two, of such momentous infamy, so unexpectedly, on that occasion of particular solemnity, and in his undetermined and haphazard mood, were crushing to his self-control and deliberation. With color rapidly rushing into his face, accordingly, and dissipating his pallor, and with rising excitement exhibiting itself in nervous action, he stepped forward and separated the little group of awe-stricken friends, who had gathered around him and Isabel, and made another effort to browbeat his accuser into silence or retraction; but, conscious of her justice and truth, his violence reacted against himself with so much force, he could scarcely speak.

Believe her not!—he repeatedly said,—believe her not!—Then added, as assurance returned to him in a measure, and a thought and line of action presented itself,—She raves! Insanity's distinctness bears the semblance of remembered truth! She raves!

But Teresa stood unmoved, and waited till Alvaro's violence had expended itself in his charge against her reason. Then, with majestic mien, commanding respect, and a firm and dignified utterance, which could issue only from the might of truth, she replied; and, in her abstract and ideal language, harrowed and cross-harrowed the soul of the guilty man, till it appeared in his countenance and action as ragged and bare as ever were broken field and fallow.

Base man, within the house of God, before His consecrated priest, with vows still fresh upon your lips, dare you to imitate the bold, unblushing guilt of Cain, and make reply unto your Maker? Hear you not the mighty waters' moan proclaim your guilt, as murdered Abel's blood did cry to God from outraged earth? And hear you not poor Isabel's wild shriek, which pierced the vault of Heaven, and there recorded her great grief and your black crime? And you to wed the one, whose love and life you crushed forever, then? Just God!

A death-like silence followed this speech of Teresa, so terrible in its accusation, so stern in its delivery, and so weird and awful in its imagery.

Isabel turned toward her father, and buried her head in his bosom.

The feeling of horror she experienced at her near approach to union with crime, of such heinous character and appalling magnitude as murder, was enough to make her shrink from Alvaro and withdraw to that haven to her of innocence, purity, and security, her father. Add to this horror, then, her amaze at the real character of Teresa and the unhallowed relationship between her and Alvaro; then cap this mountain of circumstance with her thoughts and feelings with respect to Zomara, that undercurrent of her being, which set in motion, sank all else into insignificance, and you have Isabel before you in her father's arms, sinking down,

down, even deeper in despair than ever before, and yet withal maintain her consciousness and sensibility.

What a loathsome stream of crime, flowing beneath a sheen of crystals which dazzled and deceived, was now revealed to her, when the spring time of discovery and the warm sun of truth divided and drifted away the thawing floe and the melting fragment of ice!

This is too much!—said Alvaro, as Isabel, and even his father, shrank away from him, and left him in bold relief in adjudged guilt.—This is too much! Her words burn through my soul! The world grows black as its charred mass! All that is dear gone, gone now forever!

When the human heart is laid bare, and the blackness of guilt is found to the core, to whom is the sight more repulsive, loathsome, and terrible, than its wretched, wretched owner!

His head fell upon his breast. Manhood forsook him. Even the semblance of humanity left him, and a savage monster rose in its stead—a monster that knew not pity nor sensibility; a monster that knew not sanctity in man nor God; a monster that knew no means to attain an end save destruction!

Raising his head suddenly, and expanding with the might of the monster roused within him, and standing out with the fullness and distinctness of daring and deadly passion when lashed to fury, he turned toward Teresa; and, in the grandeur of his power and fell intent, looming up like El Capitan, the poor defenceless woman sank, and hung suspended like a sable cloud far down in the valley. His features assumed the grim and remorseless outlines of a hungry lion chiseled in steel, and his motions were those of a well-directed machine, as precise, inevitable, and unconcerned as those of fate itself. And his voice, as strangely changed as form and feature, pealing forth in thunder tones, which, rolling up in mighty waves with the measured motion of martial music, reverberated in the capacious vault above, till the very cathedral seemed to quake.

Pale phantom of a dead and expiated past, why rise again to turn my hopes into statues of stone?

Why come from buried years to rake the ashes of long burnt-out joys for living coals? Oh, will you never rest? Then let the shroud, the coffin, and the heavy clod forever hold you down.

Saying which, and before anybody could divine his intent, before the altar of God, beneath the Holy Cross on which His Son was crucified, and in the presence of His delegated minister of His love and grace, he seized the dagger of Zomara, which Isabel bore at her belt, even in her bridal array, and a sight of which he caught as she turned away from him, and in an instant plunged its gleaming blade into Teresa's bosom!

The shriek of Teresa, as she staggered from the force of the blow, sent a thrill of anguish to the heart of all, which brought horror and dismay to a culminating point, and a general groan issued in sympathetic response.

But Alvaro, following up the staggering stab with the rapacity of the savage monster roused within him, strove to strike again; for he felt the blade had been illy directed in his haste at first, and had struck he knew not what, but certainly not the heart of his victim!

It was the crescent of Zomara his own dagger pierced!

Strange tokens of love and gratitude, a dagger and a crescent! Mysterious and doubtful! But as the events of this history transpire, what hidden significance their symbols reveal! Even the taint of Moorish blood in her veins, conveyed by the crescent, disappears, when, in revealing her origin and history, that very symbol, borne like a trinket on her bosom, saves her life! a shield between her and an illy directed dagger—perverted love!—and the Holy Cross of religion desecrated!—and many other interpretations, such as your imaginations may conjure up.

But before Alvaro could strike a second blow, his father, Borracho, and his good friend, the doctor, Quesada, interposed, and restrained him; seizing each an arm, and securely pinioning him between them.

Hold! hold, my son!—exclaimed the agonized Borracho.—Restrain your murderous hand, or direct your blade against your poor old father's heart at once!

And Teresa, recovering, and courting death at the hands of him whom she had loved with such intensity, and hated with such jealousy as only her intense love could be perverted into, begged him to strike again.

Stab me with steel, and end this wretched life, so often stabbed by you with shame and woe!

But the holy priest here interposed, and with the authority of his sacred ministry, commanded peace.

My children, peace!—he said, in solemn and impressive tones. Then turning to Alvaro, who had yielded to the force and persuasions of his father and Quesada,—My son, this charge is grave; but this is no place nor time to weigh it. Accuser and accused must meet elsewhere for judgment. Yield, my son, to me, and remain within this sanctuary, safe and secure, till law and justice mete out to you your just deserts. Yield, my son; the laws of man and God alike call you to account.

Alvaro kneeled before the priest, and in that humble posture remained till all were gone, even his father, and Quesada, who had become attached to him with an affection akin to paternal.

XXIII.

ALAS! our fate!—said Isabel to Teresa, approaching her as she stood alone in the cathedral, and throwing her arms about her neck, exhibiting a sense of the awful disclosures and terrible happenings of the day, if she could not compass their entirety in a single phrase.—And Teresa, or Joanna your name may be, and your life the mirror of Alvaro's evil, our past communion in friendship and love, and our kindred burdens of misery and woe, must unite us still, and even more closely and tenderly than ever.

Teresa hesitated. The demon of jealousy had separated them too far for this overture of affection to bring them together in sympathy in an instant. But a sense of her utter loneliness and desolation, without the sympathy of Isabel, possessed her, and, by degrees, the rugged outlines of repelling jealousy softened down into the yielding features of a tender woman—feeling personified, from its faintest emotion to its most intense and deadly of passions.

Teresa to you, Isabel, and to your kind and loving father and mother; but Joanna, the mistress of a murderer, in the ears and eyes of the world beside. Do you not loathe me, Isabel, when my shame is so glaring, despite the weight of woe that is crushing me, and moves your sympathetic heart to pity?

This was the last rally of her expiring jealousy, a doubt which she felt the tears of Isabel on her neck should forever set at rest.

But alas! the woe, Isabel; if not to you, to whom will I turn for that feeling which alone makes existence tolerable, sympathy in distress and despair? Even my child is cold and strange to me, my lady; wonder and doubt return my embrace and kisses when I hold him in my arms, after my prolonged absence in your service, and in my watchings, like a guardian angel I had hoped, but a demon of destruction in reality, by the side of his father! Alas! my lady, how can I meet the innocence of my darling boy with shame eternal on his mother's brow, and the damning guilt of murder in his father's heart! My child! my poor child, what an inheritance of misery is thy lot!

And tear and sob, and that oppressive sense of choking incident to the maternal feeling of sympathy, solicitude, and anxious care for a beloved child, prevented further utterance, and left her—like a tempest-tossed bark in a heavy sea—to right herself in a flood of tears.

XXIV.

THE trial of Alvaro came on apace. Confronted by Teresa, accompanied by her son, the wretched man turned in agony from their sight, and begged the judge to condemn and sentence, and even execute, him at once.

However, the trial was continued and conducted in due form. And among other evidences of Zomara's death, were the sword of Zomara, which his lieutenant had dredged from the sea beneath the cliff, when the storm abated; and the very clothes of Zomara, which he had worn on the day and night of his descent on the coast, found in a pawnbroker's shop several weeks after the supposed murder, with the very rents of the deadly blade of Alvaro, though sewed together with a hasty and bungling hand, in confirmation of Teresa's account, and in attestation of Zomara's death. The earnest and inquiring lieutenant, in the guise of a pilgrim to the shrine of Compostella, had even traced the clothing of Zomara to Barnabas, and with bribe and threat of exposure, had wrung from Barnabas the fact that the corpse of the man from whom the clothing was stripped, had been borne to the gaol with a number of pirates wrecked on the coast on the night of Zomara's disappearance, and who were all executed, except a poor, raving maniac, who, in pity, was confined in a cell, and who, of course, could neither know nor declare anything about Zomara or anybody else.

A summons was forthwith issued for Barnabas, and a messenger dispatched to bid him appear in court at once. But the messenger returned in a little while alone. Barnabas had gone on a secret mission to the king, leaving the prisoner under the charge of his brother, a deputy jailer, who had served before in that capacity, and was known to the judge as a good and honest man—the same he could not say with so much confidence of his brother, Barnabas.

The confession of Alvaro was sufficient, however. He had beheld himself the corpse of Zomara in the dungeon. He had directed Barnabas to bury or burn the clothing, and had suspected him of treachery at the time, which the clothes in witness now in court was confirmation incontestible by its circumstance and direction.

Moreover, the sacrilegious attempt to murder Teresa in the cathedral, in that holiest of sanctuaries, was glaring cause for condemnation and death, without the consideration of the murder of Zomara.

Alvaro was accordingly doomed to death, the day of his execution fixed, and the manner prescribed—the block, and, in consideration of his nobility, the execution to take place in the privacy of the prison.

He was then removed to the dungeon, and confined in a cell adjoining the one in which Zonnara lay in the apathy of despair, but double-locked and chained, and riveted to the floor, and barred and bolted in the cell from all external sight and sound, save that which entered with his keeper. A thousand gold doubloons his head was worth, and Barnabas would make it sure and safe in his absence to reveal his prisoner to the king, and claim the coveted reward.

XXV.

LET us now move forward to the fatal day, the day of the execution of Alvaro—Christmas, at his own appointment, the second anniversary of the bloody day of the murder,—and behold the doomed man alone in his cell with the priest, who had not forsaken him in his crime, but sought him again and again in the exercise of his office and mission—the confession, forgiveness, and salvation of his holy faith.

Alvaro, however, was not the man to accept absolution with perfect, passive, and unreflecting faith. Bowed down and broken, it was fate and circumstance irresistible that ruined him, not crime and evil; and he awaited his execution with a calmness which could result only from this philosophic conviction. What faith and religion there were in him belonged more to his circumstances than himself; for he was, with the entirety of his being, a doubter, and doubt is fatal to faith. But his was a character little understood by the priest, where submission passed for contrition, and indifference to faith.

That I am the betrayer of Teresa and the murderer of Zonnara, I have confessed before my judges and before you—the penalty awarded to my crimes is justly death, and I accept it. Father, I thank you for the absolution of our holy church, if the thanks of a wretch, guilty of the most heinous crimes, can be received by one so holy as yourself.

Alvaro spoke this calmly, and there was truth and sincerity in the speech, if the philosopher be properly judged; but when he is contrasted with a confiding priest, his utterances will savor of hypocrisy.

My son, your penitence and faith deserve this absolution, and will, I trust, obtain you peace in a better world,—replied the satisfied priest.

Now, usher in my father and such friends as wish to bid farewell to one who aimed to honor them and win their love, but who dishonored them and earned reproach, and who deserves to die!—continued Alvaro, in the same calm and submissive tone, and in idea and term within the comprehension of the holy man.

The priest withdrew, and left the philosopher in a reverie on death, a sequence following the suggestive words "to die!" with which he concluded his behest.

What myriads of thoughts converge to that brief phrase—to die!

What hells of woe, and heavens of bliss await a man—when he has ceased to be!

What stabs, and burns, and racks, and peace, and joy, and love, greet him—when he has crumbled back to earth!

Great world of the Unknown, Eternity, what varied homes thou givest to him—when he needs them not!

Vain speculations of far-seeing idiots!

All hail, Philosophy, that counts a being from its birth to death, and while it hears, and sees, and feels, gives it this earth of pain and pleasure here to torture or delight it!

Why don a shroud to enter heaven?
Why leap the grave to enter hell?
Here is the paradise for him that doeth well!
Here is the yawning gulf for him that doeth
ill!

Reaching the acme of religious doubt, which
the presence and remarks of the priest had forced
upon him, Alvaro crowned his philosophy with a
total abnegation of the soul, upon which the fabric
of religion is based, and launched boldly out into
the opposing theory of individual existence and
annihilation.

And while he was lost in his abstraction the
priest re-entered, and with him came Borracho,
pale and haggard, broken-hearted Borracho, and
Altanero, Lady Mariana, Isabel, and by her side,
a wan and woe-racked woman, Teresa, leading a
timid and wondering boy—Alvaro's son.

Alvaro!—said Teresa, with a faint and faltering
voice, as she approached him in his deep abstraction, his back turned to the door at which she
entered.

That voice again!—he said, as he awoke to
consciousness with a start, as if from a horrible
dream, but in this instance, from a happy dream,
comparatively, into a terrible reality. Then turning toward her with savage resignation, he exclaimed,—

Avenging fury, scourge—scourge me to the
grave!

No fury, reeking with vengeance, Alvaro,—replied Teresa, calmly,—but your wife—the mother
of your child—who wept with secret joy, when
first you stood within her cottage door, enclosed
in that rude frame the bright fulfillment of her
girlish heart's ideal; who, walking, arm in arm
with you, through leafy groves, took in with
eager ears your sweet discourse on nature's forms
of beauty, and, wondering, asked herself, why she
should thus be blest above her sex; whose heart
hung trembling like an aspen leaf, when first you
took her by the hand; whose being felt itself
transfused to yours, when first you spoke the
welcome words of love, and sealed them with a
kiss; who, when a mother's hopes first faintly
dawned upon her life, thought shame too poor a

price for the joy to bear the child of him she
worshiped as divine; who, when you coldly
threw away the love so gladly given; still followed
you with deeper, more unselfish love; who gave
to stranger hands a mother's proudest charge, in
order to obtain a hiding-place from which to gaze
on him she had so loved and lost; who, when the
hour had come to make you husband to another,
wildly uttered words the rack could not have
wrung from her, had not her reason fled, expelled
by overwhelming grief; who would now gladly
die for you, if that could purchase life for him she
ever loved and cherished through her shame, disgrace and woe.

Alvaro, with his hand across his eyes, listened
to Teresa's every word, and followed her with
imaginings of the various phases and steps of
their early love and histories to that hour, in even
brighter hues than she depicted. Her deep devotion, from the hour they met until the present,
grew upon him; and the love he once felt for her
began to revive and glow, and, as he stood in
silent meditation, his being changed, reverted to
his early manhood, when Teresa—or Joanna, as
he knew her then—was the idol of his heart.

He withdrew his hand from his eyes and looked
into her face. There were the features of his beloved Joanna; but, ah! how sadly changed! And
as he gazed he caught the tender glance of her
eyes, riveting him to her as in former days.

Joanna, forgive me!—at length he said, as he
still looked into her eyes, and spoke as if he ad-
dressed a spirit of love which was there revealed
rather than a reality; for, in fact, at that moment
of his reverie the ideal was a greater impression
in his mind than the real.—Joanna, forgive me!
if, through the misery I have heaped upon you,
a prayer, with my latest breath, can reach your
pity and love! Forgive the puppet of fate.

The solemnity with which he uttered these
words, like the sad solemnity of the occasion and
circumstances which called them forth, was most
impressive. The group stood as if carved in stone.
All eyes were fixed on Alvaro save his own, and
his were riveted in Teresa's look, till he uttered
the last sentence, when, raising his hand again, and

pressing it hard against his brow, he was left alone with the image on his brain of Teresa, surrounded with a halo of pity and love, in which she gleamed like an angel of light.

That I should be so blind! To stare at distant starry specks in the darkness of night, and see not in the gleam of noonday a sphere of love revolving in my path, worth more than worlds of senseless matter!

Teresa feared to move or speak. She knew Alvaro was contemplating an ideal, and not a real form, and she dreaded lest the slightest sound should break the spell.

Come nearer, and stand by my side, Joanna,—said Alvaro, in the piteous tone of a man stricken blind, as in fact he was blind with his hand across his eyes.

Teresa approached, but not so close as to touch him.

Still nearer, Joanna; and take this hand in yours,—extending his right to her, which she took and held, while his left still pressed his brow.

Art thou Joanna? Speak! It is the voice that reveals thee, not the wan and haggard looks that blind, and the trembling touch that chills. Art thou Joanna? Speak! Oh, speak! or leave me with this image on my brain to pass into eternity!

I am Joanna!—answered Teresa, sadly, and with hesitation; for as she held once more the hand of Alvaro, a dream of happiness for years, and found her being shrink from contact with its cold, unfeeling, and unnatural touch, she doubted the identity of Alvaro and Rodrigo, and doubted even herself, with her unnatural feelings, at that instant.

Most holy father,—said Alvaro, addressing the priest, with tones directed to the spot where he stood when he had seen him last, before he closed his eyes, as if forever,—behold before you Alvaro, of Grenada, and Joanna, of Catalonia, whom love has united, but whom the word of priest has not declared man and wife, and their issue legitimate. Before these witnesses, pronounce us man and wife, and absolve me in reality from the crime that looms up darkest in the horizon of my life.

The priest accordingly pronounced them man and wife, by virtue of the authority of his of-

fice and the rites of the most holy church; and showered blessings on them for the noble act of goodness, pity, and love, on the one hand, and love and justice on the other.

Alvaro removed his hand from his brow, looked fondly into the face of his wife, kissed her tenderly, and pressed her to his bosom. He then took up his child, and started as he beheld the lineaments of his face so strongly marked in the boy's. By nature's law he was his son. And now, by his solemn marriage, according to the rights of the church, the boy was his son and heir before any court in the realm.

Turning, now, to his weeping father, the heartbroken Borracho, Alvaro bade him receive Joanna as his wife, and the boy he held in his arms as his son, heir to all the honors, titles, and estates of his ancient family. He then kissed Joanna and the child again, and bade them farewell forever.

My daughter, come to me,—said Borracho, through his tears, to the sinking wife of the murderer, doomed to eternity in a few brief minutes.— Come to me, my daughter, with your child. The world may be harsh, but it is just: for God ruleth all. A husband to you may perish, and a son to me; but you live with a father and child henceforth, and I with a daughter and son as well.

Then addressing Alvaro, Borracho said, with increasing firmness, as his sense of justice and honor was aroused—My son, this act redeems you. Now meet your death as becomes Alvaro and his lineage, on the heels of a good and noble deed. Farewell—I will hallow your memory, not loathe it! My son, my noble son, farewell.

As Borracho received Teresa in his arms, the woe-begone woman almost fainting in the extreme exhaustion of her grief and anguish, and her child clinging to her in wild affright and terror, he stepped to one side and allowed the others to bid the wretched man a last adieu.

The most unhappy one,—said Isabel, moving toward him with the solemn motion of a spectre, and the low, sad voice of sympathy in woe,—for whom two lives, so dear to all, are given, forgives and asks forgiveness.

My lady, Isabel,—replied Alvaro, kindly,—forget the proud, imperious man of later years, and when the grave encloses him, recall him, as your gentlest friend of childhood—and the sad, repentant husband of Teresa. I thank you for your kind forgiveness. Farewell.

Lady Mariana likewise approached, and bade him farewell, uttering a prayer to which all cried Amen! a response from their hearts.

May the Christian's faith support you in the valley and shadow of death!

Amen! amen!

At this juncture the dull, dismal tling of the prison bell was heard, giving harsh and startling warning that the hour of twelve was almost at hand—the hour appointed for the sword to descend and launch the being of Alvaro into eternity.

A groan of agony responded to the terrible warning. Emotions burst into uncontrolling sway, and the fountains of tears welled up and overflowed afresh.

The time has come when you must part forever, —said the priest, maintaining a firmness in his demeanor in keeping little with his sinking, sympathetic heart.—Your last farewell is spoken!

Alvaro again embraced Teresa, his child, and his father; then turned and stood with stoic firmness, looking against the blank wall of his cell, while the fainting woman, the weeping, wondering child, and the trembling, tottering old man were removed by the kindly assistance of Isabel, Lady Mariana, Altanero, and the tender-hearted priest.

This act of justice to Joanna,—said Alvaro to himself,—draws the tearing teeth of fierce remorse. O true, exalted one, how sweet were life to be again with you! But the poverty only of death reveals the wonderful wealth of life!

How true it is, the wish is father to the thought. No sooner did Alvaro long for life, than dreams of living on, on, on forever possessed him; his doctrine of annihilation vanished; and a life beyond the grave dawned upon him, where, opposing what was dreaded here, were love, and peace, and innocence immutable for aye.

In his reverie, moreover, he reviewed the religions of man, and back, back through the lore of ages, he traced the myth of the soul, till, far away in dreamy Ind, where metempsychosis gave it direct and tangible existence, he harbored in a complacent sea at rest. And lo! the preserving deity, equal, in the trimurti of the Godhead, with the creating and the destroying powers, rises in triumph from the wave, issuing from the maw of a monstrous fish, life eternal from seeming death and annihilation!

Ah, ye who store the youthful mind with fact or fancy, know ye the power of every, even the faintest impression, on the brain? Know ye that equal there they stand in might, truth and fiction, to move and sway the course of thought and reason! rule to weal or woe the mass encompassing of flesh and blood!

What is a doubt?

What is the force impelling, in a man like Alvaro, that directs and drives him into thoughts and actions so different and divergent from those that move the masses about him?

A doubt, my children, is a fact outside the common groove, an impression outside a certain sequence, that affects the common current by contact or relationship, and affects all currents of thought, as well as those pertaining to religion.

For instance, knew Alvaro no more than what he learned from the priest, he would have been as passive, plastic putty in his hands; but myriads of thoughts from many sources crowded in his brain and wrangled there for precedence and preeminence, now one and now another in the lead, and now one line of action, and now another, mayhap in a contrary direction.

The active mind, with various and diverse facts, is essentially a doubter.

And the greatest doubter, or he who is affected in his thoughts by the greatest number of varied impressions, has attained the ultimate of wisdom.

But you grow impatient again; you will not wait till I lead you through Alvaro's thoughts, with a more observing and circumstantial tongue, and detail the sequence leading from the sea, into which Zomara was hurled to death, to the sea from which the life-preserving deity emerged, in the guise of a Hindoo fable, impressed on the philosopher's memory from the study of some sacred Vedic page. Well, well, my children, my story draws to a close, and your impatience to hear the conclusion must be relieved and satisfied.

XXVI.

WHILE the latter part of the last scene was enacted in one cell, Alvaro's, another scene transpired in the adjoining cell of Zomara, which must now be described.

Miguel, the brother of Barnabas, and the deputy jailer, to whom it fell, in his official capacity, to execute Alvaro, was too tender-hearted and timid to strike the fatal blow. He bethought him, however, of the crazy wretch in his charge, as one who, for some paltry bribe, would do the work as well as Barnabas himself, if he were at his post. He accordingly proposed to Zomara that, for an extra quantity and quality of provisions, he would behead a prisoner condemned for murder?

But Zomara, shriveled and shrunk to a shadow, and fallen into the apathy of wretchedness, gave Miguel no answer, but cast a look of such intense loathing and scorn upon him, that made him blanch and grow faint at the idea of the horrible function he must fulfill.

Miguel then offered to bribe him with gold; but the same look of loathing and scorn cut off this hope.

The jailer next offered to remove the prisoner's chains, and allow him the freedom of the hall; but the same silent denial and rebuke met him.

In despair, Miguel then tendered Zomara his liberty, whether or not he meant to fulfill his promise, it matters little.

Alas!—sighed Zomara, at length,—what boots it, liberty to me! unless it be the illimitable liberty of death.

What! cheer up, my man,—said the jailer, supposing Zomara in despondency and despair from long confinement,—cheer up! Go out and behold the sunshine! Go out, and chat and talk and laugh with your fellowmen! Go out, and share in the games and cheer of Christmas! for you must know, my man, this day is merry Christmas to all outside this dungeon's walls! Cheer up!

Christmas, said you?—asked Zomara, with interest and eagerness in his speech.

Christmas it is, my man, all the world over,—responded Miguel.

How long have I been confined in this dungeon?

How can I tell, my good man? But a long time, I'm sure; for I heard my boy tell of a crazy pirate in his uncle's charge, and—ah, he was a good child, and his father's solace and joy!—he has been dead for nigh two years.

Two years!—exclaimed Zomara.

Why, let me see, my good man. At least two years, by the mass—for, as I remember now, it was on a Christmas night, and a heavy sea was beating against the rocks, and the pirate's vessel, the Black Eagle, was bearing down into the harbor to pillage the town, when she struck a rock and split, going down with all on board. Yes, I remember well, for on the morning after the wreck I assisted in rescuing several of the pirates, and maybe you yourself, my good man, for you were all so nearly dead, you could not tell a sound man from a mad one. Yes, my good man, perhaps you owe your life to me, for—

What hour is it now, good jailer?

The signal bell tapped but a moment ago. It lacks now but a few minutes of twelve. And at twelve o'clock the murderer must be executed. The block is in readiness in the hall, and the judge

67

awaits to see that his sentence is properly carried out.

Will you remove these shackles from my feet, these manacles from my wrists, and unlock this iron band that galls my neck?

I will,—said the jailer, and forthwith unlocked the chain and collar.

But the sword must be keen, good jailer, and not too heavy for these wasted arms?

Just so, my good man; I will fetch the blade, that you may test its edge and weight.

Miguel then went out into the hall, and returned with a sword which he gave to Zomara.

This will do,—said Zomara, with satisfaction, as his nervous hand clutched the familiar weapon, and clinched around the handle with the firmness of death,—I am ready now.

But you must don this mask first,—said Miguel.—Humanity demands that the eye of the doomed man behold not the face of the executioner.

No, good jailer; I must see the neck of the murderer, else how can I sever it at a blow?

True, my man; but the mask has loopholes that you may see and not be seen.

Zomara then submitted to wear the mask, and, after its adjustment, was led into the hall, and stationed by the side of Alvaro, who, on his knees, with bowed head and bared neck, waited with calm resignation the blow.

XXVII.

EXECUTIONER,—said Alvaro, with his eye fixed on the floor of the prison hall,—make sure your blow. The guilt of your victim is your warrant. At the first tap of the bell, strike—for there are ages crowding into seconds now! I forgive you the act—it is your duty—the decree of justice. Father, your blessing. Farewell.

The priest pronounced his blessing over the wretched man, and silently withdrew a pace or two and turned away his head, that he might not witness the terrible scene.

The judge, too, admonished the executioner to strike at the first tap of the bell; then bade him be ready, and turned away to give the signal.

Zomara stood with uplifted sword above the bared neck of Alvaro!

Recall, now, the pain, and anguish, and woe, which Zomara has endured for two years in the loathsome dungeon, with Barnabas for his keeper! Recall, now, the sorrow, and grief, and misery which Isabel has endured—which Teresa has endured—and Altamero and Borracho! And see the sword of vengeance gleam as it quivers in anxious suspense over the neck of the guilty author of this accumulation of suffering, torture and agony in the extreme!

Who more worthy to wield the sword of vengeance than Zomara? Who more deserving of the blow than Alvaro?

But while Zomara stood with drawn sword, at the first tap of the bell Teresa rushed frantically into the hall, and threw herself between him and Alvaro, and, with uplifted hands, implored the executioner to stay his hand.

Spare, oh, spare my husband!—she piteously cried, in the extremity of her woe,—or let my head, with his, lie pillowed on the block in death's long sleep.

By some means, Teresa, in the madness of her anguish, had broken away from Borracho and Isabel, who supported her, and returned to the prison; and, through the negligence of Miguel, in his excitement, leaving the outer door unlocked, she had gained access to the hall at the critical moment of the first stroke of twelve, and the first tap of the bell that was to summon her husband into eternity.

Borracho, too, had followed her even into the hall; but when he beheld the sword raised above the neck of his son, transfixed with agony, he stopped in an instant, and buried his face in his hands.

But Zomara stood like a statue, immovable as granite itself, even until after the twelfth bell had sounded, and the troubled and excited Miguel had urged him with threat and menace of death itself, and the impatient judge had commanded him again and again to strike! little regarding they the prayer of Teresa, who, drawn away by the priest from beneath the threatening blade, still plead and shrieked alternate with the sound and silence of the bell!

And as the last tap of the bell died away, and Miguel, enraged, was about to seize Zomara, dispossess him of the sword, and either execute Alvaro or wreak his vengeance on his prisoner for defeating the designs of justice, Zomara hurled the sword against the floor of the prison, and declared aloud—

THE HOUR OF TWELVE IS PAST, AND ZOMARA, OF CASTILE, IS FREE!

Zomara, of Castile!—repeated Teresa, in wild amaze.—O God, can it be he!

And with one bound she sprang to his side and tore the mask from Zomara, standing motionless in abstract contemplation of his freedom.

It is!—it is Zomara!—Oh, joyful sight!

But sudden joy is as depressing to the system as sudden grief. With the declaration of the recognition of Zomara, she swooned away and sank to the floor.

She fell happily over the sword which Zomara had thrown on the floor, and prevented Miguel from securing it until the situation was the better understood; for the jailer, now wrought to a frenzy, would have run Zomara through, if he could have gotten hold of the sword at that instant. As it was, he possessed himself of the weapon in another minute, and made a desperate attempt to stab him.

What, villain! Defeat the court's decree? Defy my strict command? Receive the just reward of your treachery!

But the judge himself interposed between the jailer and Zomara, and restrained the excited man at his peril.

And Barnabas, who at that instant had returned from the king, and entered at the open door and found his brother about to stab his prize, wrenched the sword from his hand, and burst out in his usual style—

Ha! a gallus cove! to kill my prize! A thousand gold doubloons!—that's what his head is worth—ha! a gallus head! I have been to the king—here's his letter to Don Alvaro. Ha! a gallus letter!

What, to me?—Let me have it?—said Alvaro, who had risen from his kneeling position when Zomara threw down the sword, and uttered the words which declared not only himself, Zomara, free, but also him, Alvaro! free from the crime and imputation of murder! for the murdered stood revealed a living man before him!

But before Alvaro took the letter, he raised Teresa fondly from the floor, kissed her again and again, then laid her gently down, and bade his father fan her, that she might recover from her faint the more readily. He then took the letter, broke the seal, and read the missive to himself.

Zomara, now beginning to realize the situation he had been in a few minutes before and was at present,—his brain, with his emaciated form, being dull and heavy, and slow to act—began to utter his thoughts aloud, as passion was once more roused within him in the presence of his rival.

Was it Alvaro's neck beneath my sword!—he said,—the lurking spy who sought to murder me! the false friend who has wed the inconstant Isabel!

No,—said Teresa, recovering from her swoon, and answering Zomara as she lay on the floor of the prison.—Alvaro has not married Isabel, but whom you knew as Teresa. The true heart of Isabel still cherishes the memory of Zomara.

Oh, welcome news!—responded Zomara; his ears unused to any save the grating sounds of rusty locks and creaking doors, and the demoniac laugh of Barnabas, catching, for the first time in two years, the music of a woman's voice; and his being trembling at the notes which brought such hopes of love and life, both long despaired of.

Alvaro, having finished reading the letter of the king, advanced toward Zomara, and took him by the hand.

Zomara,—said he,—first let me lay a contrite heart before you, and crave your forgiveness for the mountain of misery I have heaped upon you; and know that for your supposed murder, by my reckless hand, my neck was bowed beneath your sword; but, by the decree of fate, your hand was held—the grave gave up its murdered dead; the murderer knelt a guiltless man before you.

Then know,—continued he,—that the king, learning, through Barnabas, that you were confined in his cell in the guise of a crazy pirate, and learning, from private dispatches, since Barnabas set out on his mission, that I was accused of your murder, and had confessed to the charge in my belief and conviction, has sent me this message, which declares your existence and my innocence, and your freedom henceforth, with restoration to rank in the army and restitution of the revenues of your confiscated estate.

Know farther,—continued Alvaro, directing his speech to the judge and Barnabas,—the king commands that Barnabas, the jailer, who, by his own confession, has shown so much brutality toward Zomara in his greed for gold, be forthwith confined in Zomara's cell, and be released not until so ordered by his majesty. Servant of the king, most worthy judge, witness the royal seal, and do your duty.

Ha! a gallus letter!—said Barnabas, with fictitious firmness.—Ha! a gallus fool was the jailer-king to step before a real king!

Then hummed he his accustomed air, to which it might be supposed his thoughts arranged themselves about as follows:

> Now, a jailer-king, no more I'll sing,
> For the doubloons of gold
> Did make me too bold,—
> Good-bye to the jailer-king!

And while the judge and Miguel were adjusting Zomara's collar about the neck of Barnabas, and locking the manacles about his wrists, and were leading him into the empty cell, while curses loud and vindictive began to issue from his savage heart, the priest, who had hurried away from the hall on the discovery of Zomara, returned; and in his company came Isabel, Lady Mariana, Altanero, and Quesada, and that worthy trio, Pedro, Nona, and Martin, who had come to the jail-yard for curiosity, if for nothing else.

A miracle! a miracle! come! come!—exclaimed the priest, as he hurried the wondering people into the hall.

O Isabel, do I once more press you to my bosom!—said Zomara, embracing the woman whom he so dearly loved.—How I have longed, through dark and dreary years, for this blessed hour! How I have sought with bribe and prayer to send you tidings of my escape from death! How I have suffered agonies of hell—at distant sight of you, have strained my prison bars, till strength and reason fled! But now, how changed! —peace, and happiness, and love, at last!

And I, beloved one,—said Isabel, madly happy, but, nevertheless, shuddering in the embrace of the wretched man, so grim, and grizzled, and ghastly, from his confinement and harsh treatment in the dungeon.—And I, beloved one, believed you dead, and prayed that I might perish too, and be with you beyond the grave; but, here united, we will never part.

My father and my mother,—continued she, addressing her parents, who stood in abject wonder, if not dread, at her side,—oh, greet Zomara, greet him as your son, for to him your daughter's troth is plighted through life unto death, and thence through eternity, as on the holy symbol of the cross I swear, and seal my vow with an irrevocable kiss!

Saying which, and her noble individuality asserting itself with the heroic spirit of her ancestry, she disengaged herself from Zomara's arms, drew the dagger-token from her belt, held it by the blade before her, and pressed the cross, which it formed when thus held, with solemn deliberation against her lips!

While Isabel was declaring her vow, and revealing the significance of the symbol of the dagger-cross, Teresa, catching the spirit of the enigmas with her kindred soul, took her crescent from her bosom, and, wondering, as she gazed at the symbol of light emerging from darkness, said—

So thus, thou wouldst reveal, O unsolved symbol, that in the darkness of despair the orbs of light and love still gleam on high, but, separated from our feeble ken, by clouds of circumstance, we blindly grope in error in the dark!

And the priest, taking the cue from Teresa's remarks, and extending her thoughts into the idea of his religion, which associated itself with light from darkness, added, in solemn voice—

And God said, let there be light, and there was light. His grace be with us, now and forever.

And with this pious declaration and invocation of the priest, let me bring this story to a close.

Yes, yes; of course, Zomara and Isabel were married, and lived happily to a good old age, and were bountifully supplied with blessings commensurate and compensative for all their sufferings; while Altanero and Lady Mariana, in due course of time, were laid in peaceful graves.

And Alvaro and Teresa were married again, with more becoming solemnity and pomp than in the dungeon a few minutes before the threatened execution; their son grew up a great and good man, the mother's firm and unflinching faith overbalancing the philosophic father's doubts; while the jovial old Don lived for many a day after, to laugh in rollicksome glee at the trials which ended at last in joy; and Quesada lived in becoming state and style to the day of his death, a pensioner on the bounty of his wealthy, philosophic friend.

And Nona, and Martin, and Pedro—what became of them?

Well, Nona and Martin eventually were married, during a severe illness of Pedro, who, when he recovered, was so much shocked at what had hap-

pened during his compulsory absence, that, heaving one profound sigh in attestation of the inconstancy of woman, he had expiring strength left to utter only once more the conviction of his being,—a woman's a woman the wide world over!

No, Martin never told stories to his children and children's children on Christmas-eve; but—would you believe it?—Nona entirely recovered from the sourness and rheumatism of single life for half a century, in the comforts and consolations of a decade of matrimonial existence—another proof, as Pedro would say, if he were still living, that a woman's a woman the wide world over.

And Barnabas, as you might be assured, received the just reward of his criminal and brutal conduct to Zomara, as well as to others, till, broken down and truly penitent, after several years of solitary confinement in Zomara's cell, he was released, at the intercession of the kind-hearted priest, and died a pious, humble man, a few days after he regained his freedom—before he had time to revert to his former savage nature.

Now, to bed! to bed! my children, one and all!

What! Tommy, asleep, with Tabby crooning o'er some old cat sonnet in his lap! Well, this is satire indeed! Wake up, my little man, wake up!

A SUGGESTION.

www.ingramcontent.com/pod-product-compliance
Lightning Source LLC
Chambersburg PA
CBHW030025030726
47499CB00008B/3125